# ALL THAT GLITTERS

## THE REDEMPTION SERIES BOOK 2

AMANDA J. CLAY

# PART I

---

*Approximately 80 percent of the global opioid supply is consumed in the United States.*

- *Centers for Disease Control and Prevention*

# 1

eksik Vahtra sat in his office at the Royale Luxury Casino and Resort on the Nevada California border of North Lake Tahoe. The buzz of the casinos rang in the distant background, the laughter from disillusioned high-rollers across all facets of life—dentists, lawyers, open-heart surgeons, brokers, businessmen, retailers, manufacturers—a plethora of anonymous plebes deluding themselves into dreams of beating the house.

Nothing crossed class lines like infectious greed. The scent of sin and piggish indulgence clung to the walls, infested the air.

Aaron Feinstein, President and CEO of Cerberus LTD., sat across from him, needlessly adjusting his tie. He wiped the sheen of perspiration from his greasy brow. Feinstein had an unlikeable face. Bulbous nose and bushy brows, a caricature. But the man knew his business and for this acumen, Leksik forgave a great many grievances.

Still, things had gone terribly fucking wrong and someone needed to answer for it.

"This is not personal, Feinstein," Leksik said.

Feinstein smiled thinly. His thick lips peeled at the corners. He licked them like a lizard. "Hard to believe it isn't, sir?"

"You, of all people, should know this is just business. I don't blame you for what happened. I blame my nephew, Luther. But the reality is somebody needs to come in and take a heavy hand with this. And because I have enough invested in this project, that person should be myself."

"I can promise you, Leksik, that we're on it. Fixing all the broken pipelines as we speak," Feinstein said, his New York accent thickening like paste with his nerves.

Leksik sighed. He reached for the ice bucket on his desk and dropped a few cubes into two lowball glasses, then filled them with a limited batch Viru Valge vodka. He slid one to Feinstein.

"I believe you, Aaron, I do. I am not doubting your desire to correct this mess. But it was not you who solely created it and therefore it will not be you to solely fix it. My nephew fucked things up. I know this. And I take responsibility for my family."

Leksik had always considered Luther more than just a nephew, but also a friend. Being born Czech, Luther had always been an outsider, and because he was neither Estonian nor Russian, he had to fight a little harder for his place. But his heart was all Opik. Since the wall came down, the organization was such a mismatch of Eastern Bloc misfits, it hardly mattered where one came from anymore. After Luther returned from America, he had quickly adapted to their way of life. He was an eager pupil, willing to learn anything, do anything. Nothing fazed him. Leksik had always assumed the man was a pure psychopath. He'd seen him gouge out a man's eyeballs with his finger, after all.

But then came Nina.

Nina, whom Luther needed to own, to possess. Nina, whom he could not let go. Nina, who eventually destroyed him.

Luther's climb through the ranks of the organization wouldn't have known any bounds had he not gotten involved with that woman. He was even in line to replace Leksik as head of the family someday.

But women were always the downfall of powerful men. The proverbial Eves. A story made up by men that so perfectly illustrated their own weaknesses. Leksik was aware of this weakness and for this he did not allow anything but the most carnal of interactions.

"Don't think that I don't lament the demise of my nephew, Aaron. He was a fighter, a soldier."

"Forgive me, sir, but Luther Kavka was a psychopath."

Leksik rubbed his chin gently. Were psychopaths capable of the emotional attachment Luther had formed to Nina?

He did murder his own mother. Or perhaps, he only saved Elena Kavka from a pitiful life of pain.

"It is not our place to judge the actions of others when we cannot fully understand their situation. You, my good Feinstein, have never suffered the injuries that we have. You would never have understood my nephew fully."

Aaron snorted. "You make Estonia sound like the pits of a fiery hell, Leksik."

Leksik laughed. "No, my friend. Estonia is heavenly. Golden beautiful spires, majestic cathedrals, rolling hills and luxurious estates. It is a pristine piece of Nordic paradise. But we have been abused, oppressed, torn apart by powers who would wish to own us, control us. From the days of the Vikings, our land has been a favorite toy, torn between societies. And because of this, we have known poverty and oppression and hardship in a way that you never will."

"Fucking Russians," Feinstein said, as if to commiserate. He raised his glass.

Leksik raised an eyebrow. "It would do you good not to generalize populations, my friend. A lot of people hate the Jews, don't they?"

Feinstein shrugged. "You get used to it." He took a heavy drink. "So, what now? You gonna kill me?"

Leksik laughed. "Kill you? What a stupid idea. There is a big difference between betrayal and disappointment. If I killed everyone who disappointed me, I'd have no one left with whom to do business."

Leksik tapped his pencil on the table a few times. Feinstein eyed the motion warily. A sheen of sweat covered the pudgy man's face. He could really do with a workout from time to time. Maybe stop shoveling food into his face like there was no tomorrow.

"I have a new plan," Leksik finally said, straightening his tie.

Feinstein swallowed hard, his Adam's apple bobbing. "All ears."

"I want the girl on our side. I think we should bring her into the fold."

Feinstein's face went through a span of emotion in the blink of an eye. The question danced in his eyes—was this a test? Was Leksik serious? Leksik appreciated the fear in his eyes. People didn't need to love him, but they did need to fear and respect him.

"Well?" Leksik asked after a moment of silence.

Feinstein glanced around the room. "That's unexpected."

"Predictability is a man's downfall."

"Three months ago, you wanted her dead. 'Bring me her eyeballs,' if I remember correctly. Now you want her on our team?"

"I was very angry a few months ago, Aaron. I have had time to reflect and consider. She knows a few things that we would like to know. What if we bring her onto our side and turned her against the DEA? A bit of a, what do they call that here? A double agent."

A hint of laughter tickled Feinstein's mouth. "Forgive me, but are you joking?"

Leksik met his eyes directly. "Do I strike you as the type who makes jokes?"

Terrified, Feinstein composed his expression. "No, of course not, sir. All respect and all, but she'll never turn, Leksik."

Leksik bobbed his head, sure of himself. "She will for the right motivation. She has a family, does she not?"

"Yeah, sister. Niece and nephew. You want her bad enough to go after a mom with young kids?"

Leksik offered a small shrug. "Nina might be the key to fixing this mess. Our pipelines have been compromised. Many of our top suppliers. She can get close to what the Feds know. Play both sides."

"We can't trust her. She's turned on us before."

"Did she?"

"No proof, but c'mon, does anyone think she didn't roll?"

"My nephew didn't think so. If he had thought she was a rat, she would be dead. I want everything there is to know about her. Her history, her prison time. How she likes her fucking coffee. Everything."

The door opened then, and a young woman walked in. She had strawberry hair wound up tightly on top of her head, a slender body elegantly draped in a chic black dress, and long alabaster legs concluding in sharp heels.

"Ahh, my dear," Leksik said. "Aaron, have you met my lovely assistant, Katja Vahtra?"

Katja sauntered over one hip at a time, her waltz a delicate practice, her long body lithe and slithering like a snake. The tattoo of the serpent down her arm danced with her movements. So many people wrongly assumed that women weren't dangerous. Katja was as dangerous as any man. Fire in the flesh. Piercing.

Feinstein eyed the slinky redhead with misgiving.

In the short time Leksik had been acquainted with Feinstein, the man had proved to be a misogynistic fuck who thought of women as weak, frivolous, and disposable. Leksik supposed if you spent your entire life in casinos surrounded by prostitutes of all kinds, it would be easy to develop that opinion.

But Feinstein didn't understand the women from his country. Estonian women were hardened, sharp. Formidable.

Leksik looked up at his cousin. "Katja, we were just discussing how to fix this mess that has been created by Luther's missteps."

Katja arched an overly plucked brow, looking much like an arch nemesis in a comic.

"I too am here to help," Katja said, her voice ethereal, seductive, like the vapors of an aged scotch. Her accent was back in full now that she no longer needed to pretend to be Katie, American waitress. She stood with icy majesty, a viper queen ready to take down her enemies.

Leksik supposed if he ever did intend on spending his life with a woman, she would be someone like Katja.

"And you're, uh, part of the family?" Feinstein asked.

Katja tilted her head and nodded just slightly. "Yes, I think third cousin is the right term in English. Or is it great niece? It is hard to keep track of these things."

She slid up next to Leksik and he placed a gentle hand on her backside.

Discomfort flashed across Feinstein's face, as if the people in his country hadn't been bedding their siblings for generations.

"Katja here is the best at what she does," Leksik said.

"And what is it that she does, exactly?" Feinstein asked.

Katja smiled. "Whatever is asked of me."

"She will be a valuable asset to us as we go forward. As you can imagine, she has a very persuasive way about her."

Feinstein tittered and looked less than certain. "Look Leksik, I don't really see the problem. Things ran perfectly smooth in Luther's absence before. I mean, he was dead for all parties concerned."

"But Luther was not actually gone before. He was just out of sight," Leksik said. "Look, my friend. As long as you continue on as you're supposed to, everything is going to be okay. Nothing needs to change. It didn't before."

Feinstein blinked and offered a curt nod, but his response seemed to be lodged in his throat.

Katja looked at Aaron with something like amused pity. "What did you really expect, Aaron? You made a deal with the devil. Did you expect it to be fair?"

Feinstein met her eyes. Much to his amusement, Leksik saw the unadulterated fear there. Yes, he could work with fear like that.

## 2

Howling mountain winds teased from outside. Icy rain slammed against the windows of The Black Cat Restaurant and Bar. Outside, the sky was black and thunder growled. The lake docks groaned and heaved against quays as the wind forced the water up, waves slapping and chuckling over the shore, slinking toward lakeside buildings.

The storm was gaining momentum and Nina was starting to worry about the premature winter. People often mistook California as the land of incessant summer, but this wasn't Florida. Winter in the mountains came at you full force, raging against its summer rival, determined to prove itself superior.

She watched the torrent from inside, thinking that the weather seemed to fit her mood lately—sudden, violent storms with fleeting rays of sunshine.

Sometimes she still felt the knife in her hands.

Sometimes she tasted blood.

Sometimes she felt the kick of the gun.

She closed the blinds and walked to the back of the

restaurant. She turned up the music a little louder, hoping to drown out the surging storm and the persistent voices in her head, the persistent visions of all that had transpired.

The poetry of Social Distortion flooded the restaurant.

*They'd put a price on my head*
*Wanted dead or alive or painted a bloodied red*
*For you, for you*
*Like an outlaw*
*I'd kill for you*

UNLIKE THE WEATHER OUTSIDE, LIFE HAD SETTLED INTO A gentle cadence, the daily even flow lapping against reality like the waves of the lake shore. But Nina knew better than to trust the calm. It was simply the eye of the storm.

She watched the dinner shift unfold, the workers buzzing about their routine tasks, everything in order, everything as it should be. But it was all wrong. It was like she was watching her days unfold from outside herself.

Maybe she was just having a nervous breakdown. She certainly wouldn't be the first person to suffer a break after shooting their ex-boyfriend/nemesis.

She laughed gently to herself. You couldn't make this shit up.

In her dreams, she saw his face right before she pulled the trigger. His body tumbling into the dark water. She felt the warmth of the gun in her hand. She felt the kick. The acrid taste of residue. The crisp bitter night filling her lungs.

She often woke to the smell of gunfire and smoke.

When she heard the gentle cadence of Beck's breath beside her, it gave her some solace. But then the guilt would kick in—the lies, the betrayal, not knowing who she really was, what life she was truly meant to live. It was a treacherous thing to not know your place in the world anymore. She was thirty and yet had lived so many lives already. What would her next incarnation be? Would she ever live to find out?

Maybe she was just losing her mind.

The hardest thing was that she couldn't confide in anyone. She couldn't admit there was this lingering grief. Luther had been a part of her. Now that those ties were truly severed, it was hard to admit, even to herself, that she felt the phantom pain of its loss. But how did she explain that to Beck? Or even to Brooklyn? After all, why would anyone grieve for a monster?

The therapist's business card burned a hole in her jeans pocket. She really ought to consider a session. But she didn't know where she'd even begin. *Once upon a time, I met a man who would change my soul. And then I killed him. Twice...*

Her phone buzzed, an action that might forever make her jump.

She breathed and checked. It was a text from her sister Cammy with a picture attached.

She opened it to reveal two cherub faces smiling up at her with the caption that read *We love you, Auntie!*

Nina's heart contracted. Being let back into Cammy's life had been the greatest joy she had ever known. Getting to share moments of Abby and Jacob's life, having a sister again. A pinch of salt stung the back of her eyes. She never realized she could love things so fiercely until she held those two kiddos and knew that her blood ran through them and that she'd protect them as if they were her own.

Nina knew how badly she'd hurt her family, the deep pain it had caused them all. The damage you could inflict on strangers was nothing compared to what you could do to those closest to you.

"Nina!" a teeny voice said, snapping her from her thoughts.

Nina turned to see Melanie walking in, holding her wide-eyed three-year-old daughter, Tara, who was flashing a toothy grin at Nina.

"Hey you!" Nina said, trickling the girl's tummy. "Hey, Mel. Here for your paycheck?"

"Yeah, if you have a sec," Melanie said. Her voice was chipper and upbeat.

"Hey, I bet Reina will give you an ice cream if you go see her," Nina said to Tara.

"Nina, it's 10 a.m.," Melanie said, so parent-like that Nina almost felt guilty.

"But it's raining out." Nina pointed to the window.

"That somehow makes a difference?"

Nina shrugged. "It's science. Can't argue science."

"Pweez, mom. Just a small one. This big," Tara said, pinching her tiny fingers together.

Melanie rolled her eyes and laughed. She set her daughter down. "Okay fine, but just a teeny scoop."

Tara giggled and scampered around the corner to the bar where Reina was setting up.

"She's really sweet," Nina said.

Melanie beamed. "Yeah. She's everything to me."

It had been a rough journey, but Melanie had come so far these past few months. There was a time when Nina had her doubts about whether Melanie would ever make a full recovery, get clean, and get her life together enough to be the kind of mother Tara needed. The kind of woman who could take on the world without some shitbag man like Ed knocking her around. It was the risk she took hiring recovering addicts and ex-cons—not everyone turned their life around in the end. But now Melanie's eyes were clear, her spirits high, and her mood uplifted. She was showing up to every shift, on time, with a smile. In fact, her joy was downright contagious.

It had taken courage to walk away from Ed, Nina knew that. It was easy to judge but drugs weren't the only addiction people like Melanie faced. Girls who thought they weren't good enough for an education, for dreams of bigger things. Girls who worked their fingers to the bone, met a guy, got pregnant, got married, had a couple of more kids, maybe got divorced, sometimes in that order, sometimes not. If she was lucky, the guy didn't beat her much.

Every ounce of contentment in Mel's face had been hard won.

"You seem really good, Mel," Nina said.

Melanie blushed. "I am. You know, I really am. I have to say, I've never felt so light. I've never felt so just...just good. I suppose it's because I haven't wound up with a bloody nose in a while," Melanie said with a sly smile.

Nina laughed. It was good that at least she could laugh about it. They all needed to find humor in their mistakes.

Nina was helping Brooklyn polish wine glasses when she caught a glimpse of him in her peripheral—dark thunderstorm raging in and uprooting her proper state of mind.

She collected herself, wiped her hands on her apron and smoothed her hair back, wiping the sweat from her brow.

He walked through the restaurant, broad shoulders filling out a tailored suit, catching the eye of everyone he passed. He was the kind of man who left smoke rings where he'd been.

Nina's heart picked up a beat and her lips curved into a smile.

Then she remembered she was angry with him.

She thrust the polishing rag into the sink and crossed her arms, jutting out one hip.

"Well, well, look who's here," Brooklyn said beside her.

"He's here on business," Nina said, blandly. "About the case."

"Mmm, hmm." Brooklyn said.

Nina didn't bother glaring or correcting her. She motioned for Beck to meet her in the back office.

She closed her office door and met his stormy gaze.

"I know I owe you an apology and I can see that you're mad," Beck said before Nina could start in on him.

"I'm not mad. I'm frustrated," Nina said.

"I'm sorry for not coming over last night. There was this break on the case," Beck said.

"Yeah, I know. I know all about cases and obligations and how things come up. Story of both our lives." She ran her hand through her sweaty hair, getting her fingers stuck in a snarl. She yanked it free, and along with it came a piece of spinach. She flicked the greenery to the floor. "I know better, that's the thing. I know better than to think some secret relationship between us is ever going to work."

"Nina, c'mon, don't be so dramatic. Neither of us thought this was going to be some storybook courtship. I'd say given the circumstances, we're doing just fine."

Nina snorted. "Just fine? We never even see each other. We can't even *tell* anyone we're seeing each other. That's not a relationship, that's a booty call."

Beck grabbed her hand. "Don't be ridiculous. It's so much more than that to me and you know it."

All the things Nina wanted to say threatened to spill out.

*Some days I feel like the threads of this life we have together are slowly unraveling, one small stitch at a time and we're going to wake up one day and look at the threadbare tapestry of our lives and wonder what happened.*

*I feel the divide widening between us. I feel you looking for the excuses. We fall back into our old patterns, wanting to take the easy way out and run. Light the match and pour gasoline on the flames. Thoroughly destroy ourselves so that we are forced to reinvent...*

"What are you thinking?" Beck said.

Nina ignored him and pulled away. "Has Martinez said anything to you? About us."

Beck looked hesitant then shrugged slightly. "I mean, he's given me the warnings, *in case I get any ideas*. But that's about it. He's my boss and he's a pro, but he doesn't want to kick the hornets' nest on this in the middle of a massive case."

Nina nodded. DEA Senior Special Agent Vince Martinez had always kept an incredulous eye on Nina, but he respected Beck enough to trust his judgment.

"God, it's hard to keep it under wraps," Nina said.

"One would think you'd be pretty good at secrets by now."

"What's that supposed to mean?"

Beck laughed. "Exactly what I said. You, of anyone, should be pretty good at it by now."

Nina glared at him.

"Nina, relax. I'm teasing you. I know this has been hard, but did you really kid yourself into thinking that we're going to settle into some kind of normal routine?"

Nina massaged her throbbing temple. "No, of course not. But just because we think we're prepared for something doesn't always mean that we are. I guess...I guess this is just harder than I anticipated." She wanted to tell him how it wasn't just the two of them that she was struggling with. It was everything.

"Yeah, I know. I'm doing the best I can, okay? And it's better than the alternative isn't it?"

She was honestly starting to question whether or not that was true. What did they think they were going to accomplish here? Were they just living in a dream world, in too much denial to realize the stark truths of the situation? She wasn't sure she was strong enough to suffer through another loss.

"I...I don't know. Look Beck, maybe we just need some space."

"Space? Didn't you just say we hardly see each other to begin with?" There was a touch of unappreciated sarcasm to his tone.

"I mean mental space. I spend entirely too much time thinking about us, about whatever this is. Maybe given everything else going on, it's too much."

"I think you're just stressed. You haven't been sleeping well," Beck said.

"Maybe you're just dense." She started toward the door, but Beck pulled her into a warm embrace before she could get by him.

She savored the scent of him, leather and musk. Fresh earth and grass. Without thinking, she nuzzled her head into the crook of his neck. It fit so perfectly there. God, couldn't it just be like this always? Just the two of them in some quiet mountain oasis. Nothing else in the world to distract them.

It was easy to run when things got tough. It was easy to lie to herself and pretend that she'd be just fine on her own, that this was more hassle than it was worth. That maybe she'd even be better off. But in moments of clarity, the thought of never nuzzling into his neck, never smelling the ghost of his presence on her pillow, never feeling the gentle cadence of his breath, tore her to shreds.

Nina pulled from his arms. "I have a lot of work to do. We can talk about this later."

"Anything I can help you with? I don't need to get back to the station for a bit," Beck said.

"Want to wash dishes?" She said.

Something like fear flashed in his stormy eyes.

Nina laughed. "I'm kidding. No, I'm good. Want something to eat? Go grab a booth and I'll bring you a burger."

NINA DRESSED A PLATE FOR BECK IN SILENCE, CONTEMPLATING how this was going to go going forward. They'd taken down Luther, or at least everyone else thought they had. Nina of course knew better, but she had yet to tell anyone the truth. Not even Beck.

Regardless, Luther was just one cog in the vast machine that fueled this war. They had layers upon layers of people to take down if they were really going to put a stop to this thing. But just for a few minutes, Nina wanted to believe it was all over.

They'd leaked the story to the underground about what happened to Luther. The witnesses were dead and the ones who remained hadn't seen anything or were safely in custody.

As far as anyone new, Nina had gone to Luther willingly, and the DEA had intervened. She knew she was living on borrowed time if they continued to spin these tales. But for now, it was her only option. The DEA wouldn't let her leave and she was starting to feel like a fish in a barrel.

Nina set down the plate of burger and fries and a club soda for Beck.

"So, what's going on with the case?" Nina sat opposite him. "You said there was a break?"

Beck looked hesitant to answer.

"You know this only works if you're honest with me," Nina said.

"I've never lied to you," Beck said.

"Omission is just a nicer way of lying. Keeps your conscience a little lighter."

Nina folded her arms over her chest and tilted her head in a knowing look.

Beck's lips turned up in a slight smile, but it looked more like a grimace.

"I'm not trying to keep things from you, Nina. I'm just not at liberty to talk about everything. You know it's confidential."

Nina laughed. "This whole thing is just ridiculous. I'm in this fake relationship and we can't even talk about your work, which directly affects me."

"I know it's complicated. I want to tell you everything. Trust me, I want to tell you about every second of my days. But I can't because—"

"Because at the end of the day, I'm still an asset."

"You knew it was going to be like this," Beck said.

"I just think given everything that we've been through, given everything that I've done for your department, I think I deserve a little bit of candor. I want to know what's going on. I want to be let into the inner circle."

Beck laughed. "You make it sound like a secret club with a knock and a handshake."

"It's not that far off and you know it."

Beck took a big bite of his burger, chewing slowly and deliberately, buying time with his answer. He wiped his mouth with a cloth napkin and continued.

"Nina, this is a federal investigation. It's not even my call. I'm not in charge."

Nina thought back to the hierarchy of Luther's organization. How there were people at certain levels who didn't even go to the bathroom without Luther's permission.

"I understand how organizations work, trust me. But you have to understand that I'm used to being at the top of them, not with the pawns on the front line who don't get told what the mission is."

Beck's lips fell into a lazy smile. She wanted to smack it right off. Right after she kissed him.

"I better watch out or you'll be running the DEA before we realize what happened," Beck said. He rubbed at his chiseled jaw, lightly speckled with a day's growth. "What I can tell you is that the team is putting together some kind of operation."

"Like an undercover?"

"Like an undercover."

"Where?"

"I can't tell you."

Nina folded her arms over her chest and glared.

Beck laughed at her melodrama. "I'm serious, Nina. Look, there's a really good chance that Martinez is gonna pull you in. He's gonna want your insight on this thing. If anybody knows how to infiltrate these guys, it's you."

Nina shifted uncomfortably but she wasn't surprised. When they'd debriefed her, Martinez had made it clear that her role in this thing was far from over.

"Are you okay?" Beck asked.

"I'm fine. I couldn't possibly be in any more danger than I already am. So I have no choice but to just live my life."

"You keep your gun on you?"

Nina patted her back holster.

"We should probably get you a legal one. I can pull some strings to get your ban lifted," Beck said.

Nina snorted a laugh. "Hardly see how it could matter at this point."

"Well, when your boyfriend's a Fed it tends to suit to stay on the up and up."

Nina cocked her head and wiggled her eyebrows. "Are you saying you're my boyfriend, Agent Graham?"

Beck rubbed his jaw, considering her overdramatically. "Boyfriend is a stupid term. It's not like we're twelve."

"Paramour? Illicit lover?" She said dropping her tone low and sultry.

Desire flared in his eyes, his pupils expanding.

Nina laughed. "Not right now, you animal."

"Hey, you're the one making eyes at me, woman."

"We've got work to do," Nina said, standing.

"I can't tell you anything else right now," Beck said.

"I don't mean work on the case, eedjit. Don't be such a narcissist. I mean we've got things to do around the restaurant. Eat up and come help me."

## 3

S oon Nina had to be at the station for her deposition, but she had a few minutes to squeeze in her daily search. She logged into her VPN, pulled up the TOR browser and typed in the code to access the Dark web.

She still felt dirty every time she slithered under the cloak of darkness, hiding in plain sight—it was like an alternate universe, a parallel plane where evil minds were free to roam. The wild west where nothing was off limits, and everyone was on their own.

But it was the only place she could turn in times like this.

She opened the chat and checked her messages from the previous day's feelers. She was no Lisbeth Salander, but she'd learned how to navigate the dark labyrinth with moderate skill. If Luther was still kicking around—even in the far reaches of Eastern Europe—there were people in the underground who could find him.

She waited for what felt like an hour, chewing her nails like they were the daily special.

Finally, a ping from one UpYourBlarney.

*Are you out your fecking mind?*

Nina wrote back. *Afraid?*

*Feck yeah. Going nowhere near the Estonians. Mad lot, them.*

Nina leaned back and sighed. Maybe this whole thing was a dead end. So far, even though she knew people that *could* find Luther, no one *would*. Either they'd seen too much television or Nina herself should be exercising a bit more caution. Not even her go-to contact Dom, who'd helped her clean some ciphered Opik money and provided rock-solid forged passports, had any leads.

She picked up her phone and clicked through some recent photos of her and Beck. Silly faces, googly eyes. Brilliant mountain backdrop. They had been hiking in the woods around the lake, quiet and solitary. No one to disrupt the serenity. A few moments to pretend the world had righted itself. What a beautiful illusion.

She clicked off the phone screen. It was so easy to forget sometimes that they were walking just above the bedrock of evil.

Nina closed her laptop and readied herself to head to the station.

IN THE TWO MONTHS THAT FOLLOWED THE INCIDENT AT THE lake where she had dexterously escaped Luther's clutches, taking lives in the process, it had been a never-ending stream of meetings and debriefs. She'd been asked a thousand different ways how everything had gone down, but she'd stuck to her story—the story she, Beck, and Martinez had concocted out of her self-preservation and for the health of the case. Any witnesses to the events were dead. Those who only knew that she'd been in the cabin were in custody, awaiting trial. None of them had been granted bail due to the nature of their criminal ties. Likely, they'd be dead if they were still on the outside. Nina figured they were all dead eventually, anyway.

No one could know that she was the one to rip out Badger's gullet or fire that "deadly" shot into Luther—the shot she'd purposefully missed, sending Luther floating away into the dark oblivion of the Lake. The not knowing whether or not he'd climbed out was what kept her up at night.

He was presumed dead because that's what she and Beck had reported. If Beck suspected otherwise, he hadn't let on. The dishonesty hung heavy on her shoulders.

NINA, MARTINEZ, AND BECK SAT IN THE BACK ROOM OF THE Tahoe Village Police Department. Takeout boxes and coffee cups littered the room. The details of the upcoming trials for those they'd managed to capture were posted to the cork board.

The room was suffocating, the early onset of winter sending dusty thermostats cranking. But she still had a persistent fever chill, right down to her bones.

"We definitely can't have you testify openly," Beck said.

Nina laughed. "Yeah, you think? Shit, this is like six years ago all over again. So much for moving on with your life."

"That's the thing about our greatest sins. They never really go away, do they?" Martinez said.

"It would appear not," Nina said.

"So as far as anyone is concerned, you went to Luther of your own volition. You were going to rekindle your relationship, maybe run away together. The story still sticks," Martinez said.

Nina caught the annoyed flicker in Beck's eyes.

"Right," Nina said.

"And you're positive none of those guys will be able to say otherwise, right?" Martinez said.

Nina wracked her brain, trying to summon those cloudy moments in the cabin.

"Nina, this is imperative. You'll be called on to testify and we have to know this story is rock solid," Beck said.

"They might try to counter, but no one who was there in the cabin has any clout. They're all strung-out lackeys no one would really believe. Just thugs for hire," she said.

"Surprised Luther did business with them, being the savvy mastermind that he was," Beck said. His tone was sharp.

"That wasn't business. Those guys were there to do the dirty work. The *get shit done* crew. Drug running is a grimy business. You need a whole lot of expendable muscle at your disposal. People you don't mind throwing in the line of fire as you're making your escape. The business guys don't get their manicured hands dirty," Nina said.

"Except Luther," Beck said.

Nina pulled her mouth tight. "Sometimes. He had trust issues. Wanted to be on the ground floor, watching."

"What do you know about Leksik Vahtra?" Martinez said.

Nina's blood chilled at the name.

Luther had been a threat to her soul. Leksik was a threat to humanity.

"Leksik? As in the head of the family?" Nina said. The words felt like ash on her tongue.

"The one and only," Martinez said.

Nina swallowed hard. "I...not much. He's the guy, the one in charge of it all. Operates out of Tallinn."

"You've met him?" Martinez said.

Nina hesitated. Suddenly, she was back there, in an Estonian castle, lips stained with priceless wine, draped in a borrowed dress and surrounded by some of the deadliest men in the world.

She shook her head. "Don't know him."

Martinez narrowed his ebony eyes, their dark tendrils reaching right to the center of her. "Certain?"

"Certain. Why do you ask, anyway?"

"Because he's here. In Tahoe," Martinez said.

Nina dropped her coffee cup. Black liquid coated the table.

"Shit," she scrambled to wipe it up. She breathed, trying to find balance.

"Sure you don't know him?" Martinez said, a sardonic smile playing beneath his mustache.

"Why would he be here?" Nina said.

"We can only guess to oversee operations. If he's here personally, this thing has to be bigger than we ever thought. Something he didn't trust anyone else to run," Beck said.

Nina's stomach twisted, the bile slithering up her throat like an acidic snake.

There was a knock at the door, startling all three. The door pushed open and a young man entered. He wore a suit and tie and had big bright eyes.

"Ah, Agent Shay O'Malley," Martinez said. "Please come in, sit."

The young agent looked nervous, hesitant, definitely green in the gills. His large blue eyes met Nina's warily, as though she were a tiger on a leash. Nina did her best to look feral.

"She doesn't bite, I assure you," Beck said.

O'Malley shot her a doubtful look then sat.

Nina didn't appreciate being caught off guard by new players, but she checked her composure.

"Nina, this is Agent O'Malley," Martinez said.

"I gathered. What's he doing here?"

"He's going to help us on the operation."

Nina glared at Martinez. "You said no one else was to know about this."

Martinez shrugged. "In a perfect world, but we can't keep it just us three. This is a big operation. We need more resources. You can trust O'Malley. He's one of our brightest."

"He looks twelve," Nina said, not caring that O'Malley's round cheeks flushed.

"He's older than he looks, I assure you. Undercovers always look young," Beck said.

"Undercover?"

Martinez and Beck exchanged wary glances.

"He's been working the Royale the past couple of months," Beck said.

Nina swiveled her head and glared at Beck hard. "You *knew* about this? And have opted not to say anything during all of our...*meetings*?"

"Nina, don't start. Not the time," Beck said.

She turned to O'Malley. "Nice knowing you, O'Malley,"

Agent O'Malley's face softened a little then as though he'd just been challenged to a task he'd long perfected. His mouth dropped to an easy smile, his blue eyes twinkled. Suddenly, he was transformed from awkward rookie to charming boy next door. Fair play to you, agent, Nina thought.

"C'mon, now, give me a chance, Nina. You haven't even said hello," he said.

"What is it exactly you're doing at the Royale, anyway?" Nina said. Images of the flashy resort and casino on the

Nevada border flashed through her mind. The hub of all Luther's money laundering.

"That's classified," O'Malley said.

Nina snorted. "Right, okay. Well, I can see working together is going to be a treat."

"He's been staying there posing as a trust fund kid with nothing better to do than waste money at the high rollers table," Beck said, his tone growing frustrated.

"How nice for you," she said.

"Nina here has some close ties to the Opik organization as we mentioned. She's been on the inside and can tell us a lot about how you can successfully infiltrate," Beck said.

"Infiltrate what?" Nina said.

"We've had Shay playing the tables the last few months, since you told us that's how they were laundering the money. I assume that's still your story?" Martinez said.

Nina glared at him. "It's not a story. I didn't lie."

"Wouldn't even think it," Martinez said.

"To what end?"

"I want in on the trade," O'Malley said with a shrug.

"What's your in? What makes you think they'd even hint at what they've got going on?" Nina said.

"I've gotten into the back room where the big boys play. Next step is to see if I can penetrate that inner circle, gain some trust, and learn a few things. I'm nearly there, I think."

"If we can convince them that O'Malley wants in on the opioid game, then maybe they'll let enough slip."

"Do you have any idea who these guys are, Agent O'Malley? Any idea at all what they've thrown you into?" Nina said.

"That's why I'm here meeting with you. I'm getting closer to the top, so I need all the gory details."

"This is a terrible idea," Nina said.

"I appreciate your opinion and even if I were inclined to give it merit, it's far too late for such sentiments," Martinez said. "Now, let's begin then. O'Malley, what do you know and what can Nina tell you?"

"So, these guys are like the Russians," O'Malley said.

Beck interrupted. "Don't make that mistake. There are a lot of ties and overflow from the Russians, given they were once a Soviet State, so there's definitely a hangover. Some of these guys are ex KGB and Russians who settled in and never went home. But the Estonians are their own breed. Outside of the crime families, most actually consider themselves more ethnically Nordic.."

O'Malley jotted down notes like an eager schoolboy. Nina was thoroughly impressed with Beck's accurate history lesson. And even more impressed by the charisma with which he delivered the information. He would have made one helluva professor. The idea nearly made her blush.

Beck went on. "The whole area was unstable for a long time after the wall came down. The collapse of the SU was a good thing but it left a string of countries who'd been under communist control floundering and trying to figure out how to fend for themselves. That's a ripe breeding ground for crime."

"Sounds like something out of an airport thriller," O'Malley said.

"Oh honey, it's something out of your worst nightmare," Nina said.

Beck snickered subtly. "The Estonian government has made great strides in the last few years in really cracking down on organized crime. Trafficking across the borders is getting more difficult and less lucrative. So hey, why not come to the land of promise and excessive self-medication?"

"These guys here illegally or what? Why not just have ICE pick 'em up?" O'Malley said.

"They've got work Visas, sponsored and all."

"What kind of *work* does Leksik claim to be doing?"

Martinez examined the paperwork. "Consultant. Aaron Feinstein signed off on it. New York investor, now head of the casino conglomerate."

"How is that flying?" O'Malley said.

"No legal reason to revoke it. Besides, we need to bust him here on our soil. Not just kick his ass back to Estonia."

"And this Feinstein is on the up?" O'Malley said.

"Hell no," Beck said. "Dirty as a pig. But we can't prove it. That's the point."

"You planning on wearing a wire?" Nina said. She could picture how this could go. O'Malley finally gets in, they strip him down, find the wire, then start dismembering him for sport. Martinez would get his digits back in a box.

"No. Ain't my first rodeo, sister," O'Malley said. He was a little too cocky for her taste.

"Shay worked with me on a couple of rough games down in L.A.," Beck said. "He can be trusted to do what needs to be done."

Nina chewed her lip. She didn't know why she was nervous. It wasn't her skin on the line here. What did she care if some arrogant young pup got his dick chopped off in some casino back room? *Because you're a human being, Nina. And you can't just go letting other human beings walk into the viper pit unprepared.*

"Okay, so what can I tell you to try to keep you alive?" Nina said.

"Tell us who to watch out for; where they're likely to meet. Any tics we should know about," Beck said.

Nina thought and inhaled slowly. "Aaron's an arrogant

bastard. Too caught up in his own ego. He's smart, good at what he does, but if you can appeal to his vanity, you have a chance."

O'Malley nodded and jotted down notes.

"And Leksik?" O'Malley said.

Nina's blood went a little cold. "Leksik," she repeated slowly. The words felt like ash on her tongue. "I already told you I've never met him."

"C'mon, you can give us more than that. You know *something* about him," Martinez said.

Nina tensed. What could she possibly say about a man like Leksik?

Her thoughts drifted to the few moments she'd been in his presence.

SOMETIMES, THE MEMORIES OF THOSE EARLY DAYS WERE AS clear as the images in front of her. The sights, the sounds, the smells, the tastes.

The ancient castle emerged from the Estonian countryside like a beacon leading her into another world. Gilded spires reached for the puffy clouds above while the rolling hills and forests exploded in torrents of colors all around. Nina half expected a dragon to emerge at any moment, demanding a sacred talisman as a bounty.

"It's been in our family four hundred years," Luther told her, a hint of pride in his eyes. Nina tried to picture what it would be like to have such deep roots. Like so many Americans, she was a mishmash of Europeans looking for a better life centuries ago. Part Irish, part Russian, part who knew what else, any ties she had to her ancestral home were long severed.

"It's beautiful," she said, childlike in her wonder as they stepped from the hired car and approached the front entry. Luther smiled at her innocent observation.

"No, my dear, it's not beautiful, it's enchanting. As any good castle should be." Luther grinned.

From the grand entry to the gilded staircases spiraling up to the plush, well-appointed bedrooms, every part of this place was otherworldly, ancient, of a different time. A portal to the kind of life long-lost to most. But for the Opik, they still lived and breathed the smoke of their heritage.

Nina was led to her own private quarters where she could "dress" for their dinner with the famed Leksik Vahtra, head of the family.

"I'm not sure I own anything fit for dinner at a castle," Nina said in jest but with a hint of truth. Luther had dolled her up back in Tahoe, but she felt that was more casino chic. This place demanded elegance.

Luther kissed her firmly on the mouth.

"You will find everything you need inside."

Indeed, in her closet she found a slinky dress in a black that was somehow blacker than normal—ebony and rich. Beside it was accompanying heels and chandelier diamonds, the brilliance making their authenticity apparent.

Everything fit her perfectly.

Leksik hardly spoke to her all evening. She tried not to squirm, to remain poised and elegant, with a permanent easy smile. Sexy. She was used to Luther's associates ignoring her. Most were misogynistic pigs who didn't believe women had any place in business.

But Leksik hadn't even looked at her. She might as well have been furniture.

"Don't take it personally, *miláček*," Luther said as they

fixed a drink in Luther's room. "Leksik is an important man. All of us must earn his trust."

"I don't," Nina said. "And I will," she winked.

SHE CAME BACK TO THE PRESENT, TO THE DIM ROOM AND THE cheap coffee and the rest of her life on the line.

"I don't think there's anything I can tell you that you can't read in the news," she said.

Beck gave her a pleading look, playing her heartstrings like a guitar. Jerk. "Any tics? Weaknesses?"

"Not that I know of. He's a powerful man who runs a branch of one of the most powerful crime syndicates in the world. Best advice I can give is to avoid him at all costs."

"More dangerous than Luther?" Beck asked.

Every time Beck uttered Luther's name it chilled her.

"Depends on how you define it. Luther worked for Leksik, so there's that. But he did what he wanted, how he wanted. Leksik never dictated anything to Luther. They were family. They had trust."

*Until me,* Nina thought. Was she part of the reason Leksik was here in Tahoe? To seek some kind of revenge?

"We're going to need you to stay close on this," Martinez said. "I expect you won't go anywhere?"

Nina sighed and met Beck's eyes. "There's nowhere for me to go."

The truth of her words was like a shadow creeping through her soul.

## 4

———

The scent of tomato sauce and garlic filled Nina's cabin. The sizzle of oil heating in the pan danced around her. She sipped aromatic red wine as she swayed her hips to the low hum of jazz. The buzz of the football game radiated from the living room. Is this what normalcy felt like? Cooking dinner, watching sports, sipping on red wine? Was this the scene playing out in households across America? Just a normal happy couple, unwinding from their day at work. Partaking in America's pastime, eating America's favorite food. It felt foreign to her. It was too safe, there was no sense of danger. And that safety set her on edge.

She gave the red sauce a stir, hoping it was going to turn out. It had been a while since she'd made a proper, home-cooked meal. For the last year she felt like she had eaten all her meals at the restaurant.

The drone of the game went on in the background, and Beck cheered softly. She spared him a glance through the kitchen. Dressed down from his usual suit and tie, he wore a fitted black tee shirt over dark jeans. He was a little unkempt, shadowed jaw, hair shaggy around his ears. Her cheeks warmed, and her tummy executed a subtle back flip at the sight of him.

Beck spent so much time at her place now that his smell was starting to infiltrate her walls. Her pillow smelled like him and she often lingered in the morning, so she could press her nose into it. She lived each day with this strange sense that it could all go away at any moment. Because deep in the back of her mind, she knew that it most likely would. These moments of peace would not last.

"You know? I've been thinking," Nina said as she walked the two plates of spaghetti over to the coffee table.

"That's a dangerous habit," Beck said.

Nina sat beside him on the couch. "I'm serious. I was thinking that maybe we should go away for the weekend. Get out of town, somewhere relaxing. Give us the freedom to just be with each other."

Beck pressed his lips into a tight line with a small upturn that suggested it was a smile that never quite formed.

"I'm not sure that's a good idea right now," he said.

"Why not?"

"You were there today. You saw how deep the shit is getting at work. We can't just *get away* right now."

"Oh my God, what a fucking cliché," Nina said, laughing. She stabbed her fork into the spaghetti and twirled aggressively.

"Oh come on, you're mad at me over that? It's not like I have a choice. I'm buried. Of all people, you should understand. You can hardly get to the bank you're so busy with the restaurant."

"It's calming down now. This is sort of the lull between the summer and winter season."

"Well, I'm sorry that our schedules don't line up. But I can't just walk away from the case."

"Not even for a weekend?"

"No. That's not how it works."

"There's never really a break, is there?"

"Not really, no. I think I'm eligible for a sabbatical in like, ten years," Beck said, smiling.

Nina tried to mimic the sentiment, but found her lips resisting.

Beck took her hand and squeezed. She tried to pull away, but he held tightly.

"Nina, c'mon, don't be like this."

"Be like what?"

"Fussy."

"Fussy? I'm not a two-year-old, Beck. I'm just frustrated. I never even wanted a relationship and then now that I'm actually trying, we can't even spend a weekend together!"

She shoveled the spaghetti in her mouth. Beck reached for the wine bottled and refilled both their glasses.

"I'm frustrated too. But getting frustrated isn't going to change anything. There's a reason this job has left a trail of failed marriages."

"I'm hardly looking for marriage, Beck. Think I'd settle for a date."

They both laughed then, knowing they were feeling the same thing but that there was no straight answer to the life they had chosen.

"I'll think about it, okay? See if I can't work something out. But for now, can we just eat spaghetti and watch football and try to at least pretend that we're normal?" Beck said.

Normal. That thing she tried to get away from her entire life and now craved more than anything.

Beck's phone buzzed, ripping them from the moment. He glanced down to check it.

"Shit," he said.

Nina mouthed the words along with him.

"I've gotta go."

## 5

Beck left Nina's house thoroughly annoyed. She had a solid point, but what could they do about it? They'd chosen difficult lives.

There were days when Beck felt like he'd been at war with the drug gangs for twenty years, ever since Jack smoked his first joint and fell in with the wrong crowd. Beck wasn't such a prude that he thought everyone who picked up a joint was destined toward self-destruction and an inevitable life of crime. But now that he was a little older, he'd seen the widespread evil of these dealers. They sniffed out the vulnerable ones, the ones they knew couldn't walk away. The people trying to escape, young kids who don't know right from wrong, whose brains hadn't fully developed. They knew how to exploit the most vulnerable.

Most people were ignorant. They were looking for some fun, a good party, a way to escape reality for just a few minutes. Everyone from troubled teens to high-ranking executives found solace and excitement in a high. Most of them had no idea how much that 40-bag of blow they bought on a whim to make their bachelor party just a little more fun really cost society.

No, Beck blamed the people who sat back counting the money, knowing damn well what they were doing and didn't give a shit about it.

While he was no longer sitting in undercover cars, vest in place, waiting to bust up a known L.A. crack house, no longer putting his life in the gentle balance of being made by going in on the ground floor of a long-running sting, Beck was still willing to give this fight everything he had.

His black SUV pulled up to the current scene and his heart raced. It had been nearly a year since he'd been on the ground floor of a drug bust and not holed up in some office going through strategy and paperwork. The familiar adrenaline pumped through his veins.

On the surface, the scene didn't look all that exciting. A run-down casino on the Nevada border, reflective black windows giving it the illusion of grandeur in contrast to advertisements for titty shows and $1 PBRs flashing in bold neon above.

Periwinkle sky blushed against the backdrop of the skyline. Non-descript buildings protruded from the blank, neutral landscape, concrete squares somehow reminiscent of a communist hangover.

He pulled his car up to the cluster of police vehicles and an ambulance sectioned off by yellow tape.

For so long, Beck had pushed images like this of this out of his mind and here he was, back facing down the dregs of humanity.

He pulled on his flak jacket and stepped out, surveying the scene. He easily located the agent in charge.

"Agent Graham, DEA," Beck flashed his badge. "I got a call."

The agent shook his hand. "Agent Bower. Thanks for coming down."

"So, what's the story here?" Beck said.

"Homicide. Victim is a Hispanic male, early twenties. Shooter's in the room."

"So why was DEA called in? Drug-related?"

"Looks that way."

"Gang-related? I'm not handling the cartel stuff," Beck said.

Agent Bower smiled coyly.

"The shooter's name is Andrei Stepanov, a.k.a, Sticky. Russian."

"Well now, he sounds interesting," Beck said, the various scenarios tumbling through his mind at double speed.

"Claiming self-defense. We nabbed a guy slinging pills a couple of days ago in a routine and didn't think nothing of it at first. But when we got a look at the stuff, we could tell it was high pharma grade. Turns out the guy wasn't too keen on spending any time behind bars, so he squealed pretty quick when we offered him immunity for a source."

Beck's interest peaked. "I'm listening."

Agent Bower held up a bag of the goods in question. "Says this stuff is coming in through this guy, Stepanov. He's no one too special, local dealer, but as you might guess by his moniker, he's connected to your guys. We were getting ready to call you in when we got word on the homicide."

"Today just got a whole lot better. Well done today, agent."

"CSI techs are up there now. Fourth floor."

BECK RODE THE ELEVATOR UP THROUGH THE SMOKE-FILLED casino, a skeleton of its former grandeur. He made his way down a dingy hallway off the fourth floor to a ramshackle suite at the corner end.

He flashed his badge to the tech at the door.

"You'll want these," she said, handing him plastic booties and gloves.

The room was foul, the odor of stale booze, dirty sex and metallic blood clinging to the walls. The furniture was overturned, a lamp was shattered on the floor.

A body lay in a puddle of blood. Dark eyes staring vacantly at the ceiling. Techs in clean suits scoured the area for trace.

Insane rants escaped from the back room.

Delicately avoiding stepping in anything, Beck walked into the anterior room of the hotel suite.

A man was in cuffs, rabid eyes, all but foaming at the mouth. He was clearly high and possibly had been for a number of days by the feral look of him.

"Stepanvov I take it?" Beck said to the accompanying officer.

"We haven't been able to get much out of him," the officer said. "Just a bunch a nonsense and a few choice 'fuck off, pigs."

Beck laughed. He'd make him talk. They'd have their answers.

He came closer and met Stepanov's eyes.

"Hello there. We're going to have a little chat, okay?" Beck said.

"Fuck. You." Stepanov spat out, the words slipping through yellowed teeth. He smelled of grease and sweat.

"I gather that's a favorite phrase of yours. But let's try using other words, yeah? Okay, so where'd you get your supply?"

"You think I talk to you?" he said, his Russian snaking around the words.

Beck bounced his head back and forth. "Not really, no. I imagine it'll take some persuasion." He grinned widely. "But trust me friend, we at the DEA know how to be exceptionally persuasive."

Beck stood straight and lifted his chin. "Everybody, clear the room."

The other agents and officers looked around questioningly.

Beck glared, summoning his authoritative manner. "I said everybody clear the fucking room."

His head swiveled slowly back to Stepanov. "All right Andrei, just you and me now. No wires, no recordings, no boss man. Let's have a chat, shall we?"

Beck pulled over a desk chair and faced him.

"You work for the Opik?"

Andrei remained stone-faced.

"You know Leksik Vahtra is here in Tahoe?" Beck waited for the telltale flicker in his eyes, but Andrei was a pro.

"Who?" he said with indifference.

Beck smiled. "Right. Who. You're probably too low on the food chain to know him anyway. So, let's start with who you report to."

"Only my mother and Jesus Christ." Andrei grinned.

"Who pays your bills? Keeps you in vodka and high cotton?"

Andrei snickered. "I like your style, agent. I give you points. But I'm not talking."

"Not yet."

"You don't scare me. I know American police cannot torture. It's against your laws. Pity for you."

"Torture is for amateurs. How about we make a deal, yeah?" Beck said.

Andrei snorted. "Make a deal? Sure thing. You let me go, I not kill your family."

"No, you can do better, Andrei. Look, I make deals for a living you know? How do you think I found you?"

"You won't buy me, agent."

"Everybody has a price, Andrei. Name yours."

"My life is not worth a price you can pay."

Beck raked his fingers through his hair, stopping to note that it was a bit overgrown, the way Nina liked it.

"Well then, I guess we have no choice but to arrest you and lock you up," Beck said.

Andrei shrugged. "Sure thing. I can survive a prison sentence. Perhaps even escape. I cannot survive a tomb."

Beck sighed. Run-of-the-mill this guy definitely was not. Maybe a few days in solitary would loosen his lips.

"Fine. Have it your way, Stepanov. We'll chat again soon."

<br>

## 6

After Beck left, Nina sat curled up on her couch, Toulouse purring and lost in kitty dreams on her lap. His small claws dug in and out of her arm in comforting familiar cadence. She couldn't ignore the persistent fear rooted in the deep of her gut. Stress beat against her temples, sending throbbing pain down her neck and shoulders. She thumbed through an old copy of *The Vampire Lestat* for the third or fourth time in her life.

Outside, the wind howled as winter crept closer and the Gothic tale unfolded in her mind. The fireplace danced in the corner with a rhythmic crackle, the smell of burning logs waltzing through the room. She sipped her spiced apple tea and tried not to think about the fox at her door.

She felt a little like Lestat, not knowing exactly who she was—only a shell of her former self. Now stronger and more capable, her soul more eerily beautiful, but perhaps forever cursed.

Nina flipped the old paper, and something tingled at the base of her neck. Something familiar and foreboding. Like the tail end of a dream, she couldn't quite grasp its shape or reality but somehow knew it was a signal of things to come.

A loud *thump* slammed into her door.

She yelped, jumped, sending a snoozing Toulouse flying in dismay. He landed with a thud at her feet, looked up at her and hissed.

"So jumpy, stupid cat."

Nina breathed in deliberately. Probably just a tree branch tossed about in the wind. She stood slowly and crept toward the door.

She attempted to swallow the lump in her throat, reminding herself that she didn't believe in ghosts and other things that go bump in the night.

But she very much believed in nefarious killers in remote mountain towns out for revenge. Her veins crackled with ice as her fingers brushed the frigid brass doorknob. *Don't be such a girl*, she heard Beck's teasing in the back of her mind. She smiled and turned the knob.

She thrust the door open to collide with icy air and vast darkness, but nothing else. An inky sky dotted with a scattering of diamond lights stretched out over the quiet rustic road. Nina sighed. An animal lost in the dark or a wandering vagrant. Nothing more. She laughed with relief and dropped her gaze. And saw the severed head of a bird at her feet.

Nina shrieked and slammed the door. She ran to the kitchen and grabbed a butcher's knife, holding it up wildly toward the door.

Toulouse mewed and hissed.

Nina's breath flowed out in shotgun staccato as she tried to calm herself. An animal. A wild animal dropped a carcass on her doorstep, that was all. This was the mountains, all manner of creatures prowled about in darkness.

*Some on two legs.*

She slowed her breath and set down the knife. She was losing herself to paranoia.

She sat back on the couch. Toulouse hopped back up, nuzzling into her lap. She scratched his head, finding comfort in his purr.

Her phone buzzed on the coffee table.

"Shit!" She jumped again, further agitating the cat.

Nina picked up the phone as it continued to buzz.

Blocked number.

She hesitantly unlocked it to answer.

"Hello?" Nina answered meekly.

"Nina. What a treat to hear your voice after so long," a voice sharply accented with exotic Eastern European notes transcended distance and time.

Nina's heart thrummed against her chest.

Luther.

But no. It was sharper, heavily tinted with Russian influence. Not Luther's lyrical Czech notes.

"Who is this?" she said.

There was a pause, some rustling, the distance between them long and yet short at the same time.

Finally, the voice continued. "I wouldn't expect you to recognize me. We've spoken only once before. In a land far from here, surrounded by the forests of an ancient, mythical world."

The cryptic words lulled Nina into the past, wracking her brain for the face to match the voice.

But it didn't matter if she recognized the voice or not. She already knew who it was.

"I'm sorry, I don't know what you're talking about. You have the wrong person." She pulled the phone away from her face to hang up, but the voice reached for her.

"Don't hang up, Nina." The chilling command stopped her mid-motion.

"What do you want?" Nina choked out.

"I want to strike a deal."

"How did you get my number, Leksik?" Nina said.

He chuckled. "Do you really need to ask that, my dear? Much like you, when I want something, I know how to get it."

"I'm not looking for any deals. I'm out of the game," Nina said.

"You haven't even heard what I have to say."

"I don't need to. Don't contact me again."

"Don't hang up. For your own good. I know everything about you, you see. Your place of business, where you live. Your friends, your family. Perhaps this changes things, yes?"

"It changes nothing, Leksik. I know how you work. Don't think that you can intimidate me."

Leksik chuckled. "No, I know that you are not one to be intimidated. And that's not why I called. If I wanted to threaten you, there are ways that I can do that without ever having to get involved. No Nina, I'm calling because I genuinely want to work with you."

"What? Why would you want to work with me?"

"Because I think that you have some insight and information that we need."

Nina rubbed her forehead, feeling like a doll being tugged between two children.

"You mean with the DEA," she said. There was no point in beating around the bush.

She felt Leksik's smile through the phone. "I appreciate you not playing coy with me. I know why Luther loved you so."

Loved, past tense. Not love. Meaning either Luther was

no longer with them, or he no longer loved her. Nina longed to ask, but she forced her mouth shut.

"I don't know anything useful," Nina said.

"You're going to tell me that you were not working with the DEA these past few months?"

Nina's stomach turned over in sickening waves. How much did he know? How much could he prove? Did he even want proof, or was her life already forfeit?

"I won't deny that they tried. I told them some high-level things to keep them off my case. But you know as well as I do that I didn't even know enough to tell them anything. They were wasting their time with me. I haven't had any information for six years."

"But they don't know that fully, do they?" Leksik said.

Nina's nerves stood on end. "What are you getting at?"

"If you were to come work for me, I could make it very much worth your while."

Nina shook her head fervently in vain, as there was no one to see it. "Forgive me, Leksik, but you must be out of your fucking mind. There is absolutely nothing you could offer me to bring me back."

"I doubt that's true. I would be willing to throw in a sizable percentage of things for your cooperation. More money than you would know what to do with."

"In exchange for what?"

"Information from the DEA. What do they know about us? And your help in altering their understanding about our operations."

"Double informant."

"You know the game, Nina."

"Forget it."

"Come, you're telling me that you are not tempted by the

power you had in those years by Luther's side? Didn't you thrive on that high? Don't you want more?"

Nina chewed her lip to keep any unnecessary words at bay. It was hard to keep her mind from drifting back to those moments. She'd had respect. She'd had power.

No, she didn't need that kind of power anymore. She had a business and employees and people who trusted her. People who relied on her. She didn't need people afraid of her, too.

When she didn't say anything, Leksik went on. "Don't you want your freedom?"

Freedom. The only thing she ever wanted. "I have freedom. The moment I set foot back into your world, I forfeit that freedom to you."

"That is shortsighted thinking, my dear."

"Just leave me alone. It's over. Find someone else."

"It will never be over. You know that, Nina. You are Opik for life. I'm offering you your old life back. Don't you miss it? Do you really want to slave away, serving the masses for the rest of your life? Come back, and you can be a queen once again."

She felt her composure cracking under the weight of his rhetoric. "What exactly is it that you expect me to do?"

"Get that young gun at the DEA to confide in you. And then report all that information back to me."

"So you can kill everyone involved? No thank you."

"My dear, I am not an animal. I don't believe in pointless murder. But the more we know about what they know, the more we can fine-tune our operations to avoid detection. Thus, limiting bloodshed all around. That's really what you've always wanted, isn't it? Luther did mention you are quite the pacifist."

Nina's heart raced, and her palms dripped, coating the

phone with a slick sheen.

"I need time to think about this," she said.

"Of course, my dear. I wouldn't expect you to make a rash decision. If I thought you were that kind of person I would not consider you for the job."

She sat in silence for a moment, the phone pulsing in her palm.

Finally, Leksik said, "My dear, I must go. Don't go changing your number or anything. Because I will still be able to find it, but it will take me time and that will really annoy me. And you must know one thing about me my dear, I hate to be annoyed. *Hüvasti.*"

The line went dead.

Nina slowly hung up the phone and set it on the table. She leaned back on the couch for a moment, catching her breath. Then she stood and went to fetch the bottle of whiskey. She hurriedly flung off the cap and tipped it down her throat.

This couldn't be happening.

She fetched a tumbler and filled it up.

Was this all just an elaborate ruse to kill her in some creative way? If they wanted her dead, why wouldn't they just take her out? There was no way he was telling the truth, was there?

She wouldn't be the first asset to pretend to cooperate with the DEA and then secretly feed information to the other side.

But the truth was, she didn't really know anything. Despite their pillow talk, Beck was careful about what he told her. She knew he trusted her, but there was still a certain level of unease between them.

A violent torrent twisted her stomach.

Nina ran to the bathroom and threw up.

## 7

"I don't understand why you want her," Katja said in Estonian. She leaned back on the red settee by the hotel suite window and stared down at the glittering lakeside panorama below. The rain was coming down in thick, hazy sheets, casting an eerie sheen across the mountainous backdrop. She took comfort in the icy landscape and was pleasantly relieved to be rid of the oppressive summer. She had always felt more at home in the snow.

"Don't let your jealousy cloud your judgment, Katja," Leksik said, not looking up from his laptop.

Katja guffawed. "Jealousy. You don't know her like I do. I've spent time with her. She's weak. Too emotional. Malleable."

"How very human," Leksik said dryly.

"Exactly. We're wasting our time with her. Not to mention asking for trouble."

Leksik looked up and sighed. "We need more than just stone-cold killers in our employ from time to time. A little emotion could be to our benefit when it comes to getting people to cooperate."

"So now we reason with people?"

Katja drained her champagne glass then absently extended it toward the attendant standing in the corner who instantly refilled it.

"Katja, I value your opinion, but in this matter, you have no say. Get with the program."

Katja bit her lip and said nothing more. What was the big deal about this stupid American girl, anyway? She came from privilege. Upper-middle-class American idealism. Flat screen TVs and family vacations to Hawaii. All bullshit.

She didn't have the grit. She hadn't suffered nearly enough to understand. So she had a few rough years, served some time in some cozy American jail. Katja had been living in a prison her entire life. And she was sick of it. She was sick of being an animal in a cage. She was ready to run the circus.

Katja's life hadn't been easy, but she wasn't complaining, either. She had learned at a young age never to complain because so many people had it worse. The East side of Tallinn was not an easy place to grow up. As a whole, the country was safe, yes. But in her small niche, where Russian crime thrived, it had been a jungle. Being part of the organization had not been a choice, it had been survival. But it had strengthened her until she formed bones of iron. Her threshold for withstanding the fires of this world was higher than most.

"She will betray you," Katja said.

"I've heard enough, Katja. If I want her, I will get her. Is that clear?"

Katja forced a smile to mask her fury. Nina didn't even have to be present to control the men in her life. She was like a succubus, her siren song clouding their logic.

"Whatever you say, my love," Katja said. Leksik shot her an annoyed look at the term of endearment. Katja smirked.

"You're a dangerous woman, Katja. You know that, don't you?"

She smiled and sipped her champagne.

"You like it."

"Your father would have been proud. You are very much like Ivan."

Katja smiled thinly at the compliment. Her real father had died for the organization—a true hero. He had seen the world for what it was. And he knew how to take what was owed him. She still heard his words in her young ear—*Be strong. Take shit from no one. You can do what any man can do.* Katja didn't understand why her sister hadn't learned these things. Katerina had been a weakling, easily succumbing to the hardships. Katja watched her flounder and fail, bending to the will of men, only to end up in a low-end brothel, strung out and on the verge of demise. But Katerina was no longer her concern. If she wanted to waste away, that was her problem.

Katja would not bend to the will of men.

That did not mean she did not give respect where respect was due, man or woman. Leksik deserved her respect and she supposed even Luther—despite his blatant weakness—deserved an ounce or two of her allegiance.

But Nina did not. Nina was a toy, a plaything that had the men momentarily amused. A tool to be used and discarded. In Katja's opinion, Nina had long worn out her usefulness.

"Thank you, uncle," Katja said. "If you allow me I will prove to be your best asset. Let me prove my worth to you, Leksik."

"You are young. Be patient. Do what you do best for now."

"And what is it I do best?"

"Provide charming company to my enemies."

Katja snickered. "La femme fatale."

"The very best."

Katja set her drink down on the small side table and met Leksik's gaze. He was twice her age, hardened and ruthless, but he was the one thing in the world that could thaw the ice inside her.

She leaned back, exposing her pale neck.

Leksik let out a low grumble, reading her sign. He stood and moved toward her.

She saw him harden through his suit pants.

"Out," Leksik snapped to the attendants, who quickly scrambled to obey.

He turned his attention back to Katja. He loosened his tie.

"Come here," he said.

Katja arched her brow. "No. You come here."

Leksik grunted. He stopped in front of her.

"Turn around."

"No." Katja said defiantly.

Raw desire flared in his dark pupils.

He leaned down and sank his teeth into her neck. She gasped from the pain, delighted in her need for it.

With dexterous force, he thrust her knees apart and took her there on the settee.

## 8

There were days when Nina woke to the soft cadence of Beck's breath and the gentle whisper of the mountain breeze outside when she thought that everything was right in the world. Maybe life could go on normally as it should. Just two people working hard, trying to hack out a living on this crazy planet.

But then Nina would roll over and she would see the muscle and sinew of Beck's form lying beside her, his chest rising and falling as he dreamed nightmares not yet unfolded. She would take in the tattoos and deep scars and picture their origin. In those moments, the reality of her situation would come crashing back down. They were not normal, and they never would be. They would not simply exist in this world like most people did. They were broken things, perhaps set up for failure before they'd even begun.

Beck stirred beside her in bed, his breath warm on her bare skin. He reached over to pull her close, pressing his lips to her neck. She turned to him. One of his eyes fluttered open and he met her gaze.

"Morning," Nina said softly. Beck's mouth played with a

small smile.

"Good morning," he said, his voice weighed down with sleep.

"Bad dreams? Nina said

"How'd you know?"

Nina shrugged. "I can always tell."

Beck sighed and closed his eyes. "Yeah, I'm prone to nightmares."

"Have you always been?"

"Since Jack died. And then once I came back from the Middle East, they morphed into something more grotesque."

Nina wanted to say something comforting but there was nothing to be said. She knew about nightmares. And she knew nothing anyone could say would make them better. There were some things in life that just haunted you forever. She closed her eyes and nuzzled into his warm body.

"What was it about? Was it that we had to wake up and go to work?" Nina teased.

Beck was silent for a minute, his breath heavy.

"That Luther came back. And that you went with him."

Nina's eyes shot open. Tension snaked down her limbs.

"Don't be ridiculous. Luther's gone," she whispered.

Gone. Not dead. Gone.

"I know." Beck ran a trail of soft kisses up her neck. His fingers stroked her arm, gently tracing the intricate artwork dancing along her forearm, grazing over the colorful phoenix feathers.

"What was it like?" he said.

"What was what like?"

"Life with him."

Nina pressed her eyes closed and tried not to conjure the vivid memories.

"Why? It doesn't matter," she said.

"Just tell me. I'm curious."

Nina sighed and let her mind wander back through the dark labyrinth of her past. "It was exhilarating. Unpredictable. Dangerous."

"Sounds exciting."

"Until somebody gets killed. We like the idea of danger. We like the notion of our lives being on the line, the adrenaline rush that goes right up our veins, straight to our heart. But when your life is actually in danger, it becomes far less fun."

Beck smirked. "Yeah, I've had my life in the balance far more times than I'd like to admit."

"It wasn't all bad, though. What I mean by that is, while Luther gave me this pathway into a dark and dangerous world, which definitely excited me, there were also things that were glamorous, luxurious. Fine clothes, dining, luxe hotels in Europe. It was the kind of exciting life that boring little girls from boring little suburbs dream about."

"I'm not sure all little girls dream about being a mobster's girlfriend," Beck said, laughing.

"No, that's true. My sister certainly never did. Or if she did, she certainly wouldn't admit it."

"You know I make a government salary, right?"

Nina laughed. "Yes, I'm aware of the pay scale of our fine federal agents. What's that got to do with the price of tea in China?"

"I mean, you know one day I could make a comfortable living if I climbed the ranks but it's never gonna be five-star hotels in Paris money."

Nina stroked his jaw, finding comfort in its sharp edges and the feel of stubble; the fine creases where life's obstacles had left their mark.

"I've already been to Paris." She smiled and pulled him close into a kiss. He wrapped his arms around her and pulled her in.

"At least we'll have freedom," Beck whispered.

Her body stiffened. Suddenly, she heard Leksik's cold voice in her ear.

She pulled away.

"What's wrong?" Beck stroked her bare shoulder. She wanted to pull the sheets over her head and hide. She turned over and met his eyes.

"Nothing."

"Nina—"

"Just restaurant stuff. It's been a down week, so I've just been a little nervous about finances."

Beck gently pulled her face around to look at him.

"I know we haven't known each other forever, but I know you well enough to know when you're lying."

"Can we talk about it after coffee?"

Beck eased his body closer, pressing skin to skin, pressing into her breasts. He stared into her eyes, searching.

"Tell me, babe," he whispered.

Nina closed her eyes and sighed. "I got a phone call the other night."

Beck waited.

"After you left. When you got the call for that drug bust."

"Okay. From whom?"

"From," Nina paused. "From someone within the organization."

Beck pushed himself from the bed. His jaw was tight. "What? Did they threaten you?"

"No, not exactly. He...wanted something—"

"Who?" Beck demanded.

"Leksik."

He pulled away and blinked. "Leksik. I thought you didn't know him?"

The reality of her lie twisted into a hard knot inside her.

"I don't. And I don't know how he got my number, but these guys can find anyone."

"And why would he be calling you? What did he want?"

"He wanted to strike a deal. He wants me to work for him."

Beck laughed then, incredulous. "Work for him? How?"

"How do you think, Beck? He wants information on you, the case, the DEA. He thinks I can give it to him."

Beck's jaw fell slack.

"I'm not going to, Beck!"

Beck sat up taller and rubbed sleep from his eyes.

"Okay, start telling me the truth, Nina. You've at least met him."

"Okay, yes. I met him once in Estonia. He's Luther's uncle. I'm not even sure if it's a direct uncle or like a great uncle. I have no idea. Everyone in the family is connected by weird blood relations and marriages."

"You lied to me."

"No, I didn't lie. It was more of a half-truth."

"That's still a fucking lie, Nina!"

"I meant it when I said I don't know him. I mean, he didn't even speak to me. I don't even think he looked at me."

"But he sure remembered you, didn't he?"

"Beck—"

"God, I just thought maybe with Luther gone, maybe you'd actually be safe for a while. Have a chance to breathe."

Nina laughed. "No one is ever safe. Once you're a part of this thing, it's with you always. Opik are like vampires. It's like I'll always have their blood in me."

Beck got out of bed and slipped on his jeans.

"We need to go to Martinez," he said.

"Absolutely not." Nina grabbed his arm.

"You're actually thinking about..."

Nina shook her head. "No, of course not. You think I have a death wish? But if we go to Martinez, this is just going to become a thing."

"Nina, it's already a thing. You think just because you killed Luther this is over with?"

Nina narrowed her eyes. "No, this thing will never be over with. We both know that."

"Then why are you still here?" Beck said.

"Excuse me?"

"Why didn't you just run when you had the chance? Get somewhere safe."

"Because I'm done running. Why are *you* still here?"

"Because I don't have a choice. It's my job."

Nina furrowed her brow at him. Was she expecting some profession of love? Tha*t she* was the reason he was still here?

Beck took her hand and squeezed. Confusion, regret, and fear all waged war on his features. But he held steady. She squeezed his hand back.

"I'm here by your side, you know that right?" Beck said.

"I don't know what good it does," Nina said.

"It means you're not alone. It means I'm here to protect you. Not that I think I can do a better job of it than you."

Nina laughed, wiping a rogue tear from her cheek.

"I wanted to tell you. I didn't want to keep secrets. I just had to find a way to tell you," she said.

"I appreciate that," Beck said, his words clipped.

"But if you go to Martinez, I don't know what he'll do and I just—"

"Nina, stop. I'm really glad that you told me. But you understand that I have to go to Martinez with this. He's my superior. I'm under obligation. This pertains to the case and it's really serious. If Leksik wants you to come work for him that means...well, I don't know what it means exactly, but he's up to something. You understand that I can't keep that from my boss."

Nina blinked. In her effort at complete transparency with the man she was romantically involved with, she had overlooked the small detail of his professional obligation.

"But you don't understand," Nina said

Beck sighed and sat back down on the bed, pulling her with him. "Nina, I think you're the one who doesn't quite understand. This isn't a matter of just morality. This is the law. I'm a federal agent. I have a legal obligation to report everything I know about this case. And I'm sorry if that means putting you in a rough spot."

Nina ripped her hand away.

"I guess I shouldn't have told you, then."

"What? No. Of course you should have."

"But this is how it's always going to be, isn't it? We're always going to have this thing between us. I'll always have to choose between being honest with you or having you backstab me."

Beck threw up his hands, her volatile shift knocking him off guard.

"I'm not backstabbing you. Don't reduce it to that. You know it's not that black and white. It's complicated."

"Yeah, complicated. I know all about complicated."

"What is wrong with you? Are you about to start your period?"

Nina thrust herself up and yanked on a long tee shirt.

"I have to go to work. See yourself out."

She stormed into the bathroom and slammed the door.

## 9

"Beck, good morning," Martinez said before Beck had even sat down at his desk.

"What?" Beck snapped. He fell into his chair and thrust a mug of coffee to his mouth, wanting to hide his face, not wanting to confront the day.

Martinez sat across from Beck. "Wrong side of the bed?"

"Something like that." Beck's eyes avoided his boss's probing ones.

"What's going on? You look like you're about to tell me that there's a bomb under my desk," Martinez said.

Beck rubbed his stubbled jaw, four days' growth proudly residing there.

He couldn't take back what he was about to say, but he had no choice. Let the band-aid rip.

"I, um, spoke with Nina this morning," Beck said.

"Already huh? It's," Martinez checked his watch melodramatically, "barely seven."

They had an unspoken understanding about the Nina situation. Don't let it interfere, don't let anyone in the Agency find out, and Martinez kept his lips sealed.

Martinez didn't want Beck off the case any more than he did.

"Yeah. Early risers both. She had some interesting news," Beck said.

"All ears."

"She's been contacted by the organization." Beck inhaled deeply. "By Leksik Vahtra."

Martinez's draw jaw dropped an inch. "You're shitting me."

"I wish to God that I were, Martinez. He called her cell. He wants her to come work for them."

Martinez leaned back in the chair, his expression incredulous.

"Them?"

"The organization."

"I don't understand. How did this happen? Why would he get in touch with her?"

"I guess he knows her after all." Irritation at her omission stirred sour and acidic in Beck's belly.

"Well, shit, this girl has more reach than we ever knew," Martinez said, almost amused.

"Yeah, tell me about it."

"Agent Graham, you cannot let this cloud your judgment. This changes nothing."

"It doesn't?"

"Look, I'm sorry your girlfriend is a dangerous fucking criminal, but you're the one who climbed into bed with her, not me."

"She's not—"

"Save it, Graham. I don't care."

Beck's cheeks flushed but he couldn't argue. He'd damn well done this to himself.

"I understand that, sir. It won't cloud anything."

"Good. Okay, we need to figure out what to do next. How we can use this information before Leksik makes a move."

Beck cleared this throat.

"With all due respect, sir, I don't think this changes anything. We already knew he was here in Tahoe."

"You fucking kidding me? This changes everything. You think the main boss of the Opik crime family would bother with Nina if they didn't have something massive happening? That means there's multi-millions on the line here. And for all we know, Nina's in on it. She could be playing you."

Beck's gut tightened, and his cheeks burned. He gripped the desk with both hands. "He's just trying to use her as a pawn. Get info on our case. She's not in on this."

Martinez snorted incredulously. "Yet to be determined. We can use her to our advantage."

"I knew you were going to say that."

"Of course you did. Because whether you want to admit it or not, you had the same thought. You're a good agent, Graham. The best thing that we can do is send her in. Put her in undercover, let her play both sides. Just as Leksik wants, but we beat him to it."

"This is insane."

"Many of the best plans are."

Beck said nothing, gnawing his lip until he tasted metal. He licked it away.

"You don't even know whether she'll agree to this. When I talked to her, she was pretty adamant against it."

"I can be very convincing."

"Why would we think Leksik would trust her? Wouldn't it be better to send in someone clean?"

"Think about it, Graham. People are instinctively more inclined to trust people they already have a history with, a rapport, even if that history is tainted and strained. Nina spent years with his nephew. She's practically family already. We send in someone new, it could be months, hell a year, before he gets inner circle. Look how long it's taken O'Malley to break in."

Beck sighed and raked his fingers through his hair.

"C'mon, Graham, don't you trust her?"

"Of course I trust her. That's the problem. She'll disappear into that world, likely do a better job of it than any undercover we have."

"And you might lose her," Martinez said.

Beck stayed silent.

"You think she's going to be too involved in this. That in an effort to do things to the best of her ability, she'll compromise herself. And the two of you, whatever it is that you have together, as well."

"She will."

"She will. Because that's the mark of a good undercover," Martinez said.

Beck nodded. "Yes sir."

"And you want to take these guys down, right?"

"Yes."

"Then I think this conversation is over, Graham. Call in O'Malley. Let's get the brief going. No time to waste."

## 10

Nina slammed the door of the Black Cat as she entered. So what if she really was PMSing? She still had the right to be pissed off. Or just really, gut-wrenchingly frustrated and scared.

She could just leave town. She sighed. That couldn't be her answer to everything.

And while Beck had gotten her passport reinstated, she knew she could easily be flagged at the border if she fled without permission.

"Morning Nina," Brooklyn said, her tone ever chipper, regardless of the ghost of damage hanging over her head.

Brooklyn had been different since the incident with Luther. When Luther's men had kidnapped and assaulted her in order to lure Nina to him. She was recovering well, and all the physical signs had long healed, but there was a certain darkness in her eyes now. Some of the light that radiated from her core had been dimmed. It broke Nina's heart every day to see it. She knew it had been her fault and there was absolutely nothing she could do to change it. She wasn't even sure she could make amends.

Brooklyn swore everything was fine and that she didn't hold Nina accountable. But it wasn't that simple. When people suffered trauma, they needed someone to blame. Because they either blamed someone external, or they blamed themselves. And that kind of blame could erode a person's soul.

"Hey you. You alright? You look tired," Nina said.

"Don't you know you're never supposed to say that to a woman?" Brooklyn forced a thin smile. Her makeup was uncharacteristically smudged. "I'm fine. Just had a late night with Mikey."

"How are things going with him?" Nina asked.

"They're okay. They're fine."

"You don't sound so certain."

Brooklyn shrugged, averting her gaze. "I don't know. It's not like we're serious. I mean...it's nothing."

"You've been dating like, three months now, right? Still not sure about him?"

"It's hard to explain." She tucked a rogue tendril of blonde hair behind her ear. "I just—do the men in my life have to be so disappointing? God knows I don't have high standards."

"Maybe that's your problem," Nina laughed. Brooklyn's blue eyes darkened. "Hey, B. What's going on? You seem..." *Like a shell of your former self*, Nina wanted to say. "Troubled."

Brooklyn shrugged, her shoulders trembling slightly.

"I just...it's sort of hard to explain myself to him. It's hard to connect because I fear...I fear opening up. You know?"

"Because of your past?"

"Partly that. He knows a bit about it. But also, just the thing that happened to me with Luther. I just feel..." she bit her quivering red lip.

"Damaged," Nina finished the words. It wasn't a question.

"Yeah, I feel damaged. Fuck, so much as happened to me in my life and I fought so hard to move past it all. My shit family, the drugs, the bad decisions, all of it. I was finally starting to feel like a normal human woman again. Someone who might have a shot at this life after all. And I guess now I just feel like trash again."

Nina grabbed her hand and pulled her close.

"Don't you say stuff like that, okay? Don't you ever say that. What happened was not your fault. It's no reflection on who you are. It's those worthless shitheads who're trash, okay?"

Brooklyn fell into Nina's arms and made a sound somewhere between a laugh and a sob.

"C'mon, Nina. Luther saw me as somebody he could do that to. Just one of those girls no one cares if anything happens to."

"No, the complete opposite. Luther saw you as someone close to me. He knew I cared about you. He was trying to hurt *me*. It had nothing to do with the kind of woman you are. Or ever were. It's because people care about you that it happened."

Brooklyn pressed her lips into a taut smile. "Silver linings? Thanks, Nina. It's nice of you to say that. Maybe in time I'll understand that as well."

It broke Nina's heart to see the aftermath of her mistakes manifested in those she loved. But maybe it was time she stopped blaming herself and started blaming the assholes who thought of women as disposable. Brooklyn might look like she was falling apart, but Nina knew what she'd been through. She was far more resilient than most would ever be.

She trudged back to her office and plopped down at her desk. She pulled up the schedule and cross-checked that everyone had clocked in. She could hardly believe that after everything she was still having to worry about menial things like Melanie showing up for work on time. Damn it, and she'd been so good lately, too. But twenty minutes late without a text was unacceptable.

She hated to say it, but this had to be the final straw with Mel. She felt for her, she really did, but if she couldn't rely on her, then she couldn't employ her. Nina had bigger things to worry about than filling shifts at the restaurant.

She looked at the schedule, trying to work out how to rearrange the sections. Maybe it was about time she made Reina the full-time manager and gave herself a moment to breathe.

She dialed Melanie's cell. It went straight to voicemail. Something cold settled at the base of her spine. Melanie would never let her phone die—it was practically an appendage.

Something wasn't right.

She headed out front where the other girls were putting the finishing touches on their opening tasks.

"Hey, has anyone heard from Melanie today?" Nina said.

No one had.

"Everything okay?" Reina asked.

Nina rubbed her neck, trying to calm the tingling sensation.

"I'm sure it is. Her phone's just going straight to voice-mail. Kinda weird. I just...I think maybe I'm going to go check on her. Make sure she's all right. Reina, can you watch things?"

"Sure thing."

~

NINA DROVE HER JEEP TO MELANIE'S RUNDOWN APARTMENT AT
the south of town, trying to keep the panic at bay. She just
hoped Melanie wasn't sitting in a pile of her own vomit,
strung out, her kid crying.

She climbed the steps to the second floor, ignoring the
broken beer bottles and cigarette butts. Rap music blared
from one of the units. She knocked on the front door, but no
one answered. Something shuffled inside. Florescent light
peeked through the blinds. The low hum of the television
whispered through the cheap walls.

Nina's heart picked up the pace. Why hadn't she brought
her gun?

She knocked again but still no one came.

Without evidence stronger than instinct, she knew
something was terribly wrong. She breathed in and tried the
knob. It turned freely in her hand. She pushed opened
the door.

"Melanie?" Nothing. "Mel, are you home? Everything
okay?"

She assessed the apartment. It was musty, smelling of
rancid food, body odor and old beer. Cans littered the floor.
Haphazard strings of white powder and clusters of prescrip-
tions bills decorated the coffee table. She closed her eyes
and fought down the anger. If that stupid woman OD'd,
God she'd kill her.

A muffled voice whispered down the hall. She followed
it.

Nina burst through the bedroom door and nearly
collapsed. Her breath tightened. For a moment she was
pinned to the door.

Melanie was against the wall, her forehead smashed in, her body limp. Her eyes two vacant pits.

Her three-year-old daughter wept softly beside her.

Tara looked up at Nina with wide doe eyes slick with tears.

"Mama," she whimpered.

"Oh my God, Tara," Nina cried. She ran to the little girl, scooping her up in her arms, pressing her face into her chest. She knelt and checked Melanie's pulse. Nothing. Her skin was cool, ashen. The blood on her head was hot. Fresh.

Nina fumbled to get her phone out of her pocket and dialed 9-1-1.

"*9-1-1, what's your emergency?*"

"Someone's hurt. Um, Village Apartments, apartment 205," Nina rattled off.

"Hurt? What's the nature of the injury, ma'am."

"I think she's dead—"

"What the fuck are you doing here?" A male voice bellowed out. Nina shot up, dropping her phone.

She stared up at a man, tall and lanky, overgrown facial hair, faded torn work shirt over ripped jeans and biker boots.

Ed. Melanie's boyfriend. Tara's father.

Nina's insides burned with red hot, unadulterated rage. She clutched Tara close to her chest.

"What did you do to her?" Nina said through gritted teeth.

"None of your business, bitch. Get the fuck outta my house!" he bellowed.

Tara started to wail.

"And put my fucking kid down, cunt."

"Back away, you bastard." Nina took a step back, holding the child tighter.

Ed looked down at Melanie's lifeless body. His face suddenly contorted into a form of sadness. "I didn't mean to. I didn't. She...she was...fucking yelling. I didn't."

"Daddy," Tara sniffled, her small lower lip trembling with fear and confusion.

"Give her to me," Ed said.

Nina pulled the girl closer. "Not a chance. You're not going near her ever again."

"You bitch," Ed lurched toward her, but Nina jumped back. Tara whimpered. "It's okay, sweetheart. We're going to get you somewhere safe."

"I didn't mean it," Ed pleaded.

"Tell it to the cops, asshole."

Tears pricked at the back of her eyes as the reality set in.

Melanie was dead. Ed had finally killed her.

Nina might have prevented it. If only she'd taken it more seriously, intervened somehow. And now, this little girl was going to grow up without a mother, without parents. Forever confused and guilty and unsure of herself in the world. Forever feeling that heavy weight of blame.

The tears trickled down her flushed cheeks before she could stop them.

"I will kill you," Ed said. He came closer and Nina kept backing up. Her heart raced, her pulse pounded in rapid staccato against her flushed skin. Panic settled in as she realized she had backed herself into a literal corner. She assessed the room, calculating how to skirt around Ed, who was most definitely drunk and high out of his mind with nothing more to lose.

"Don't make this worse, Ed. Think of Tara. You don't want to hurt her anymore, do you?"

"Mama," Tara said on cue. The child looked down at

Melanie's disfigured body, but Nina whipped her face away and pressed it into her chest.

"Don't look, sweetie. It's going to be okay. Ed, get out of the way. Let me get Tara out of here. She needs to get somewhere safe."

"You're not going anywhere. You ain't fucking taking my kid nowhere and you sure as shit ain't calling the cops. I'll kill you first."

"Yes, we've established that," Nina said, keeping her tone even. She needed to keep him talking and not acting. She had no idea what kind of adrenaline and dope-fueled rage coursed through him. He could have been on a four-day bender for all she knew, starved and rabid.

But before she could think of another thing to say, Ed lunged for her. She shrieked and jumped out the way, but he grabbed her arm. He flung it open, forcing her to drop Tara.

"Run, Tara! Get out of here!" Nina shouted.

Tara hesitated for a split second and then bolted from the bedroom in a fit of shrieking sobs.

Ed tackled Nina, throwing her into her back. Nina screamed and kicked but Ed pinned her down.

"Stupid bitch! You were always interfering!" He revved back and smacked her across the face.

Her head hit the carpeted floor and for a second, Nina saw stars. She kept struggling, fighting to keep Ed off balance. He was high enough to not have his full wits about him, so she rocked her hips back and forth, nearly toppling him off her.

"I'll gut you," Ed said with such animated vitriol it nearly made Nina laugh.

His stale, sour breath on her face reminded her of the reality of the situation.

He moved to reposition himself and Nina saw a window.

Clenching her abs, she tilted her head back and flung herself up, slamming her own head into Ed's. He yelped and toppled off her in a fit of shouts.

Nina jumped up, dizzy and stumbling. A moment later the front door burst open with the incredible words, "Police!"

Nina stumbled out into the hallway and pointed, words barely forming on her tongue.

"In there."

Then she fell against the wall.

## 11

Nina sat in the police station of Tahoe Village PD yet again, but this time to be questioned over the death of her employee. No, her friend. For all her troubles and difficulties, Melanie had been a friend. A kind-hearted person struggling each day to do the right thing by those she cared about. And she was doing well. She'd come so far, and Ed had ripped that away from her.

The dark cloud inside Nina swelled.

"So, Melanie Baker worked for you, is that right?" said a Detective Miller.

Nina couldn't shake the image of Melanie's bloody face, her disfigured skull, a backsplash of blood on her dingy walls.

"Yes, she has—had—for a couple of years." Nina sipped the cheap coffee from the paper cup.

"Was she well liked?" Miller said.

Nina blinked, trying to make sense of his words. "Well-liked? Yes, I think so. I mean, she was a little flighty as an employee and sometimes she was a complete flake, but she got along with everyone just fine. She was kind."

The detective rubbed his jaw for a moment. "Was she using?"

"Why does that matter? If she was high she deserved it?" Nina snapped.

"That's not what I'm saying. We just need all the facts."

Nina sighed and massaged her temple. "I don't think so. She'd struggled to stay clean for a while. But she'd been clean for a couple of months as far as I know. She was trying so hard. So fucking hard." The tears welled up and Nina struggled to keep them back.

"And you don't know what exactly happened between Melanie and Ed Fowler?"

"I can guess. Melanie was always having problems with him."

"What kind of problems? They had a tumultuous relationship?"

Nina chortled. "Tumultuous is an understatement, detective. He used to beat the living shit out of her on a regular basis. He was a piece of crap addict. Couldn't get clean."

"She kept going back to him then? Why?"

"C'mon, detective. You know why. Typical abuse patterns. And they have a daughter together..." Tara's innocent face flashed through Nina's mind. "God. Tara. Is she okay?"

"She's fine. She's with her grandmother now."

A ripple crept up Nina's entire body. She had known this was inevitable. *Goddammit, Melanie!* She wanted to scream at her, shake her, tell her. But that time had passed.

"Has he been charged with her murder?" Nina said.

"Not yet. He's awaiting arraignment."

"*Will* he be convicted of this?"

"You know I couldn't speculate on that. But we'll do everything in our power to get justice for Melanie."

Nina nodded, trying to keep her chin from trembling.

Detective Miller stood. "We might be calling on you as a character witness."

"Whatever you need," Nina said.

Miller smiled thinly, regretfully. "I'm very sorry for your loss."

Sorry. Sorry didn't mean anything. Nina wanted action.

"NINA," BECK SAID, THE START OF A SCOLDING ON HIS TONGUE. "I know this is terrible, but there's nothing you could have done."

The fire crackled in the corner of her cabin, the wind rustled outside. The rain tapped gently on the window.

"I could have reported him," Nina said. She curled up on the couch, pulling her knees into her chest. Beck came over and pulled a throw blanket over her.

"You know as well as I do that it wouldn't have changed anything. He would have just come after her harder."

"She's dead, Beck. I couldn't have possibly made it worse and I *might* have helped. I could have saved her—"

"No. You couldn't have saved her. Melanie had to save herself. I know it's harsh, but she chose to stay with this guy. She chose to be an addict."

"Have you ever taken anything? You know, like a painkiller?"

Beck's jaw fell slack. "Yes. Back in the army I tore my rotator cuff. They prescribed me hydrocodone."

"The good stuff."

"Yeah, it definitely was."

"So you see how it happens, right? You're in pain. It takes the pain away. We all want to take the pain away, Beck."

"But you have to see that life is more than pain," Beck said.

"For some people, it's not. For some people life is all pain."

Beck sat beside her, placing his hand on hers. He gently stroked her flushed skin, fingers lightly running over her rough knuckles, cracked and busted from long hours washing dishes and scrubbing the bar.

"Nina, I'm not blaming her, but you can't blame yourself, either."

Nina ground her jaw. "There is someone I can blame at least."

"Don't do anything stupid. You have to let the police handle it. There's a process."

"The police didn't do shit to help her before. You know how many times they were called out there for domestic disputes?"

Beck rubbed his jaw.

"I know. I'm sorry. This is tragic. And I know the justice system can be slow, but he'll be charged and he will pay. Don't you dare get involved in this."

"I should've killed him."

"Don't say stupid things like that. You can't go rogue vigilante on this. Ed's a drugged-out loser with zero defense. He'll spend the rest of his life in jail."

Nina's body pulsed with anger, but she knew Beck was right. Still, the pain of knowing she could have helped, could have somehow saved Melanie from herself, boiled up from the core of her.

"But it won't bring her back." A tear rolled down her flushed cheek. Beck brushed it away tenderly.

"I know this is painful. It's a brutal way to lose someone."

"How many more?" Nina said.

"What?"

"How many more people will die this way because their boyfriends are too high to give a shit about anything?"

Beck sighed. "We can fight all we want, but we're never going to remove all the evil from the world. You can't stop people from using and you can't stop people from hurting others."

"But we're trying, aren't we?"

"Yeah, we're trying. It's why we wake up and go to work every day. Thinking today might be the day we save just one Melanie. And hey, to me, saving even one is worth it."

Nina pictured Melanie's face—always frantic and struggling. Hair frizzy, tired eyes. But always a gentleness about her. She'd been good at the core, wanted to do the right thing, to show her daughter a better way. And she'd come so far. But she was the victim of her own demons. Nina certainly knew what it was to be your own worst enemy, self-sabotaging. How the small voice inside you whispers that you'll never amount to anything else. That you're destined to suffer at the hands of others.

If only Nina had tried harder. Wasn't that the story of her life?

"I want to go under," Nina said.

Beck stiffened and pulled away from her. "What?"

"I want to go back inside. With the organization."

Beck's eyes flashed with fear as they considered the possibilities. She knew what he was thinking. All the same scenarios were running through her mind as well.

It was madness. Yet, she had this urge to make things right. She knew it was only the tip of the iceberg, that for every victory they would only face another defeat. This organization was deep and wide and ever replicating itself. Like a hydra, they'd cut off his head and it would only grow two more its place. It never ended.

But she had to try.

"Absolutely not," Beck said.

Nina met his eyes, the shade of a winter storm. "You don't get to make that choice."

"You're reacting emotionally. I know you're upset, but that's not a reason to risk your life."

"Then what is a good reason, Beck? My life is already at risk. Both of ours are. It's not like you're safe. Every single day you put your life on the line. You expose yourself to some of the most dangerous people on this planet."

"So just because you have to worry about me, you want me to worry about you?" Beck smirked.

"I'm not being vindictive here, Beck. I'm doing my part. If you'll recall, you're the one who dragged me into this four months ago. Let me see this thing through."

"You don't know the first thing about going undercover."

Nina laughed. "Now, that is a completely ignorant statement. Essentially, I spent three years undercover. I went from being boring, middle-class Nina to an international drug dealer. If that's not an undercover transformation, I don't know what is."

Beck was silent, his eyes regretful. "This isn't your burden."

Nina smiled thinly. "The war on drugs. Hasn't it taken enough people close to us? I might not be directly responsible for Melanie's death, but I'm guilty by proxy. I profited off of innocent lives. And now I need to join the fight. Put these motherfuckers out of business." Nina tightened her jaw. "Call Martinez. Tell him I'm in."

## 12

The nightmare was relentless. Nina struggled to wake up, tangled up in her sweaty sheets, desperately trying to break through as though she was drowning beneath a frozen-over lake. But the darkness held her close.

Finally, she snapped free with a start, sweaty, her heart pounding.

She reached for Beck beside her, finding his side of the bed cold and empty. Then she remembered. He was angry with her. Had been for days.

She remembered that Melanie was dead.

She was going in undercover.

She felt her existence contract and expand, like a lung struggling to breath.

Beck didn't understand where she was right now mentally. It was hard for her to explain. How could she tell him what she'd done at the lake still haunted her? She had fired the gun at Luther and she had purposefully missed. How could she possibly explain her twisted torment? The feeling of that piece of her finally being gone forever, and feeling the hole with phantom pain?

Maybe that was the real genesis of her grief —not just that she had lost Luther, but that she had lost part of herself in the process.

She pulled herself up and tried to shed the heavy cloak of tormented sleep.

Despite her exhaustion, her fear, there was still work to be done. Life would not break for her mental state.

THE STATION ASSISTANT LED NINA INTO THE BACK ROOM OF the station.

She had no illusions about the dangers of what she was about to do, and she didn't believe for a moment that Leksik had her best interest in mind. But she was ready to face them all down.

Beck, Martinez, and O'Malley sat at the square table, discussing charts in low voices. They all paused and looked up when Nina entered.

Martinez smiled. Beck looked ill. O'Malley looked far too sure of himself.

"Nina. Glad you're here," Martinez said.

"I'm ready. I'm ready to go in," Nina said, her words rapid, not sounding like her own.

Martinez smiled and nodded. "So Agent Graham tells me. I'm thrilled to hear it."

She met Beck's eyes and caught the anger and pain warring in their depths. She quickly averted her gaze.

Martinez motioned toward a chair. "Have a seat. I've had the paperwork drawn up for the operation already. Before we get into this, I need to ask you if you understand the implications of all of this? Are you of your sound mind, under no duress, in making this decision?"

Nina took a deep breath, exhaling slowly and audibly. She nodded.

"One hundred percent. Trust me, I know exactly what this is and what this means. And I'm prepared. I know I could get hurt."

"You could get more than hurt," Beck said. She forced herself to look at him.

"I know. I could get killed. But that's the way it goes, right? The way for evil to persist is for good people to do nothing."

"I couldn't have said it better myself," Beck said dryly.

He pressed his lips into a tight smile, one miles away from that gripping grin that could bring her to her knees. Would she ever see Beck smile like that again?

"Where do we begin?" Nina said.

Martinez rubbed his jaw thoughtfully. "We have to prep you to go under. But we'll have to work quickly. Leksik will want an answer and it's my understanding that patience is not his strong suit."

Nina nodded along, all the scenarios racing through her mind.

"I think I know what to do," Nina said.

"You've never been an official undercover. There's a protocol that goes along with it," Beck said. His tone was sharp, unforgiving.

"I'm ready to do whatever I have to do."

"You may not know this about our dear agent Graham," Martinez said. "But he was our lead undercover for years in L.A. He was pulled out to specifically work this case. What he says is gospel, and I expect you to listen to everything he says."

Nina smirked. Beck must love that part.

"We're bringing in a prep team. We'll resurrect your old persona, give you an airtight backstory, an alibi. All bases need to be covered," Beck said.

"So, basically go back to where I was when I was with Luther," Nina said.

Beck grimaced but he nodded. "Essentially. But you also have to show some growth. You can't be the exact same person. You've lived a lifetime since then."

*Don't I know it,* thought Nina.

NINA GOT BACK TO HER HOUSE UTTERLY DRAINED, BOTH physically and mentally. She dropped her purse by the door and haphazardly kicked off her boots. She made a beeline toward the kitchen and filled a glass to the brim with red wine.

She took a long sip, lit a fire, and collapsed onto the couch. Toulouse jumped up onto her lap and settled in, digging his claws into her arms.

"I know. I have been a terrible mom," Nina said, rubbing the cat's head. Toulouse mewed in agreement. Tears welled at the back of her eyes. She choked back a sob. "I'm just...I'm just not cut out to take care of others I guess."

"That couldn't be further from the truth."

Nina snapped up in a fright.

Beck stood in the doorway, bathed in the honey glow of firelight. "You left the door open."

"I thought you were angry with me," Nina said.

Beck sighed, deep and longing. "I am. But I'm also proud of you. I'm only angry because of what I stand to lose."

Nina's heart clenched. They all stood to lose so much. "Come in."

Beck stepped in and closed the front door, shutting out the rest of the world. Nina wanted to believe they could hide out in her little cabin in the woods forever.

"Drink?" Nina said, standing. Her nerves danced, and she had a hard time meeting his eyes. It was as if they hadn't shared a hundred intimate moments in the past few months. Everything felt so different now. Felt broken.

"No," Beck said. "I don't want anything right now but you."

He took an aggressive step forward and grabbed her waist. He pulled her close.

"Beck, I—"

"Shh, Don't. Don't talk. Just be."

Then his mouth crushed hers. He tasted of safety and warmth and hope.

His teeth gnashed against hers, and she fought back. Biting, grating, growling. Animalistic urges bubbled up from the pit of her, spilling out of her mouth and into his.

Suddenly her clothes felt too tight, too hot. She needed them off. She needed his skin against hers. Dizziness swirled, and her knees buckled out from under her.

He lifted her up with ease. His mouth never left hers as he carried her into the bedroom and thrust her down on the bed. Then they were tearing at each other, grasping, breathing, pulling. In organized chaos they ripped each article from each other, piece by piece, until his bare chest pressed against her swollen breasts, begging for his attention. She couldn't think, couldn't process anything other than the raw need, the pounding of her heart, the blazing heat of her skin.

His gaze, dark and dangerous, locked with hers. She

ached for him. Needed him. She raised her hips to him. Slowly—painfully slowly—he raked his gaze down the length of her body. He swallowed, his blue-gray eyes turning black with lust. Her hands ran along the sinewy torso decorated with rugged black hair. The stubble scraped her skin as his lips found every crevice of her skin. Her mind was a cloud. She could only focus on the feel of lean, sculpted muscles beneath her touch. The heave of sultry breath. Large, rough hands spanning the pale canvas of her skin.

All reason spiraled into a vortex of oblivion.

Beck lowered his mouth to her breast, teasing her nipple eagerly. She felt his arousal, hard and pulsing against her hip. Her body opened for him—ready, desperate, needing all of him.

He fisted her hair, tilting her head farther back, as his other hand slid down her spine. Her lips burned as his tongue pushed its way in to dance with hers. He was everything passion should be—raw, animal emotion erupting from his core. He tightened his grip on her waist and pulled her body closer until she felt they were melded into one another.

"I want you," he whispered against her pulsing neck. "I need you right now," he whispered into the darkness, sending shivers through every vein. She never knew before then that your entire body could throb.

She nodded desperately, barely able to speak. His knees pressed hers apart and he settled on top of her. He slid one hand around the back of her waist and lifted her hips from the small of her back. He slid the other hand beneath her shoulders and pulled her to him with urgent tenderness. He pressed his chest against her and captured her mouth, keeping his lips locked on hers as he thrust into her.

Nina cried out and he echoed with a low grumble of

desire. She lost all conscious thought as they slid into ecstasy.

AFTER, THEY LAY IN THE GLOW OF THE WANING LIGHT. SHE gazed into his reflective stare, utterly lost in the depths of his eyes. She never thought she could be so enslaved by a dangerous gaze, like hooks right to the soul. When he smiled, it brought her to her knees. She wanted every inch of his body infused with hers. Wanted every moment to be together.

She couldn't get enough of him. She was tired and sore, but she didn't care. She didn't want to sleep. She wanted the ache, to savor the pain. She wanted him in her, his weight on top of her. She wanted to feel his sweat, his heated breath. To stay in this moment forever.

But they were living on borrowed time.

Beck had to return to work with the promise that he'd try to come back if he wasn't kept there all night.

After he left, Nina was unable to sleep. She sat alone in the living room with her meandering thoughts. Partly fear, partly anxiety, partly a strange sense of excitement. Did she have any right to be excited about any of this? She was caught somewhere between two worlds. Part of her needing to just feel normal, feel like she could live in the world with other people. But then the part of her that knew she would never be normal. She would never go to an office job, get off at five and meet the girls for happy hour. She would never attend office Christmas parties and Sunday backyard barbeques. Maybe it made she and Beck the perfect pair—two people who wouldn't work well with most of society.

She slipped on her low motorcycle boots and headed off to the lakeside trail to clear her mind.

She didn't know when, or if, she might ever wander freely down these roads again. She roamed the sleepy streets, bathed in the pearly glow of moonlight. When the town was quiet, the gentle lap of waves floated up from the lake through the corridors.

The apocalyptic weather had subsided and now the fall evening was cleansing and brisk. Soon the snow would fall, the winter winds would strip the autumn leaves clean. The evergreens would stand through it all, proudly watching over the village, basking in winter glory.

The Lake Tahoe area was typically a safe place, or at least the tourist brochures liked to boast it was. *This ain't no Las Vegas!* And it was mostly true—the reigning kingpins liked to keep the violence to a minimum and stay under the radar. Deaths were usually the result of teenagers and young men performing various acts of stupidity.

But like anywhere where poverty meets tourism, bodies were occasionally found. She recalled a few grisly tales. Once a girl had been buried alive by a jealous ex-boyfriend. A few years back, a man strangled two prostitutes on the Nevada side.

Nina made her way down the woodsy path until she met the lapping shore. She sat on the grassy knoll, reveling in the serenity of the night. Fall had always been her favorite time of year—the calm before the winter tourism rush flooded the town, leaving them no respite until April.

She turned over her arm and stared at the artwork on her forearm. Intricate twists and curves, brilliant colors dancing in the moonlight, forming the family crest of the majestic Phoenix. It had hurt, burned, but she had savored the pain. It had been raw and real, injecting her with life.

She supposed that's why people got addicted to tattoos. There was something strange about the voluntary pain, standing completely still while someone jammed a needle in and out of your skin. There was some level of insanity to it, and in the moment you think, God I must be crazy. Then eventually, the burn spreads throughout your body, then your skin numbs, and your body falls into shock, a sort of quiet euphoria takes over. You slip into a ghostly place, somewhere between the two worlds of reality and dreams.

She had thought about getting it removed so many times, and maybe should have, but it would've left her horribly scarred. She wasn't sure what was worse, scars to remember her pain or this beautiful, blaring image of who she used to be.

Something cracked behind her. A branch. She shot up.

Standing not two feet behind her was a man in a dark suit and sunglasses despite the blanket of night.

Her blood ran cold. She swallowed a thick lump but didn't stand.

The man came closer, cool and collected. He said nothing. He sat beside her.

After a moment, he spoke.

"It's a beautiful place," he said through an Eastern accent. "There is a lake in Estonia, Lake Peipus, that reminds me of here. On ze border of Russia. So much life, so much death. Beauty and pain all together."

"Who are you?" Nina asked, gazing out on the blanket of navy water, glittering in the moonlight.

"He wants your answer."

She waited a beat.

"Yes," she finally said with little inflection.

The man's head turned to her. She saw the slight arch of eyebrows over his sunglasses.

"Just like that?"

"I've had days to think about it. And something happened that ushered my decision."

"Yes?"

"A friend of mine. She died. Violently, tragically. Unfairly. And it made me realize that this world is a cesspool. What's the point of any of it, really? We fight to work, to live, to scrape out some meager existence. And then we die for our trouble. I want out of this mundane life. And Leksik can give that to me."

"For a price."

"For a price."

"Mr. Vahtra will be happy to hear this."

"I imagine he won't be surprised."

"No. He is used to getting his way." The man stood.

"What happens next?" Nina asked.

"Come to the Royale in three days. Bring nothing with you. All will be provided. Make sure to tell your DEA friends."

He turned to walk away.

"Wait, I—"

He turned back and waited for her question. What did she need to know? What did she really *want* to know? A thousand thoughts ran through her mind, but she couldn't form one substantial question.

"See you in three days, Cat."

Like an apparition, the man faded into the darkness.

## 13

Nina's jeep strolled down the sleepy back roads of Tahoe Village, the grand sequoias and dirt trails bathed in the gentle glow of oncoming twilight.

She curved around the lake, the water exceedingly clear in a fan of blues from aqua to cerulean to cobalt, a bright blue eye staring upward from its granite socket like an outsized parody of Picasso. Jagged granite mountains, some already snowcapped, soared above her.

But for all the beauty surrounding her, Nina couldn't shake the case. She'd be lying to herself if she didn't admit she was wracked with fear of going under. She was also fearful of Beck getting too close—both to the organization and to her. What if she only got him killed?

The gated community of Emerald Gates rose on the horizon.

She had made such progress rebuilding a life with her family. And now, she was marching off into the unknown, possibly never to return. It was selfish and unfair to convince her family she'd changed; that she'd be there for them, that she could be someone they could rely on, and then disappear. It was unfair to those kids to introduce a new love to their life and rip it away. They were too young to understand.

Cammy was likely going to hate her forever for this, but Nina would try to make her sister understand she was doing this on behalf of the good guys. She was doing this to keep people like Cammy and her family safe.

She pulled her Jeep up to the pearly gates of the bourgeois community and gave her name to the security guard. He eyed her warily, eyes darting over her mountain chic ride and its fresh coat of mud. With obvious disapproval, he acquiesced and opened the gates.

Nina exhaled and entered a world of pristine landscaping and perfectly manicured lives. She drove along the peaceful streets of the sterile community where children rode expensive scooters down well-paved sidewalks and well-pedigreed collies lounged on Kelly green lawns dotted with impossibly pink rosebushes and City Council signs.

Nina pulled into the last cul-de-sac in the neighborhood and pulled up to the last house at the end—faux Victorian grandeur, marble statues, perfect sterling rose bushes and a quaint cobblestone walk-up.

When they were growing up, Cammy would constantly thumb through design magazines and walk through the neighborhoods with grand houses. She'd had an eye for pretty things even as a young girl and now she finally had the bankroll to create the life she'd long crafted in her mind.

It was a strange contrast to the life Nina lead. So calm. So secure. So sheltered. Nina wasn't exactly sure how she felt about it. On the one hand, she was happy that her sister, niece, and nephew were snugly tucked away in this warm little community, sheltered from the horrors of the real world. But on the other hand, on a base level, it angered her.

It angered her that people could live like this, so cut off from reality. Indifferent to the suffering of others, ignoring the dark, parallel universe just outside the gates, a world void of gray areas where good guys wore white hats and villains had sinister mustaches.

Perhaps it was only Nina's jaded self talking. She'd been forced to face those realities in the past decade of her life and there was part of her that was angry Cammy hadn't.

Part of her was just angry at herself for inflicting those things on herself. She'd made her choices, and she had to live with them.

Cammy's husband Kent greeted her at the door. He wore a fitted black sweater, dark jeans, polished brown loafers. Neatly gelled sandy hair, bright blue eyes—a walking commercial for the American dream.

"Nina," he extended his manicured hand and smiled with calculated coolness—polite but his tone well-crafted to subtly let her know that he was merely tolerating her presence.

"Kent," Nina said, trying to keep her enthusiasm up. She was so grateful to be rebuilding her relationship with Cammy and the kids, she wasn't going to let Cammy's stick-in-the-mud husband sour it.

"How lovely of you to be here," Kent said.

Nina snorted in mutual understanding at his undertones.

"Please, come in." Kent stepped aside and motioned for Nina to enter.

Nina had a hard time taking Kent seriously. Sure, he was a good guy, honest, reliable. But he had zero grit. He'd never really lived and therefore all general life advice and acumen that wasn't about personal finances seemed plucked from an HBO drama.

Even before Nina had gotten mixed up with Luther, she and Kent had always had a level of strain between them. Ever since Cammy had met him at their swanky private college at some pretentious wine and cheese nonsense, there'd been tension between them. He came from stock just high enough to feel superior to the rest of them, but not so high that he didn't still feel the threat of the *lower classes*. Nina represented a menace to his well-balanced life.

She was trying to like him. He was a provider, he was safe. He did the right thing and played the part of husband and father well. Cammy had always desired the kind of life Kent could provide—country club membership, PTA, and taking in her kid's Little League games. Whatever good qualities he had for her sister, the idea of spending her life with a man like Kent made Nina's skin crawl. He was the very definition of square. He didn't like people to think outside the box, let alone step outside it. He liked numbers and straight lines. His world existed in a pallet of neutrals.

"Awntie Nina!" Jacob's little voice said as Nina stepped into the marble entryway.

"Hey, monkey!" Nina said, scooping the four-year-old boy into her arms. She nuzzled her nose into his blonde head, savoring the fresh, innocent scent of him.

"Did you bwing me something?" Jacob asked.

"Jacob, honestly," Cammy said, her pale pink heels clacking along the marble of the entryway. She was a modern Grace Kelly in her elegance—caramel hair swept up into a chic twist, feminine A-line dress and pink lips.

Nina laughed and set her nephew down. "I sure did. How about we wait till after dinner though?"

Jacob grinned, gap-toothed and precious. He'd been born while Nina was in jail so hadn't even known his aunt existed for the first couple of years of his life. Cammy hadn't even shown Nina so much as a picture of him until she'd gotten out and then still refused to see her. She'd only known her niece and nephew for a couple of months now, but she already felt like she'd die for them.

"Glad you came," Cammy said. She gave her sister a light hug that bordered on awkward. They were still working through nearly a decade of estrangement.

"Thanks for having me, sis. I mean it." Nina and Cammy shared a brief smile. "Where's Abby?"

"Oh, I just put her down for a nap. She's climbing up on the terrible twos." Cammy shook her head dramatically.

"What can I get you to drink? Want to crack open a couple of beers?" Kent said. He always had a way of speaking to Nina as though she were *one of the guys*. It was as though when women didn't exude overt femininity, Kent wasn't quite sure what to do with them.

"Oh, whatever's open," Nina said. She felt nervous and far too accommodating.

"I just opened a bottle of wine. I'll get you a glass," Cammy said. She scurried off into the custom kitchen and Nina heard the faint swish of wine being poured into glasses. She momentarily returned with two balloons well-filled with aromatic white.

"Let's adjourn to the sitting room, shall we?" Kent said.

Sitting room. Nina was half afraid to touch anything.

Kent led the charge into a room plucked straight from the Restoration Hardware modern collection. They all three sat on the white suede couches embracing a marble coffee table. Nina clutched the wine glass with two hands, suddenly feeling like the clumsy child destined to spill in the grown-up room.

"So," Kent began. "How are things, Nina? Keeping out of trouble?"

He smiled but there was a malevolent twinkle in his eyes.

"Trying not to," Nina said. "How are you? How's the titillating world of accounting? Catch any nefarious numbers lately?"

Kent smiled sparsely. "You're looking thin."

Nina cocked an eyebrow. Kent was always great at saying the most awkward things.

"Yeah thanks, been working a lot. Probably forget to eat half the time."

"Sampling some of those diet pills?" Kent said.

"Jesus, Kent," Cammy said. "Are you going for the record of most awkward comments in an evening? I mean honestly, you have the worst social tact. You're like a wild animal."

Cammy shot Nina an apologetic look.

Nina held back a laugh. *Wild animal* was the last way she would describe her square brother-in-law.

"It's all right. It's not like being called thin is an insult after all, right?" Nina met Kent's dark eyes directly.

"Oh, I nearly forgot. I have snacks," Cammy said, nearly tittering. "Be right back."

Cammy shot up and scampered off.

"You don't have to look at me like that," Nina said once Cammy was out of earshot.

"How's that?" Kent said, sipping his wine

"Like I'm something you tracked in on your shoe."

Kent shrugged but didn't deny or qualify.

"I've never asked you to like me, Kent. But you do have to tolerate me because I'm Cammy's sister whether you like it or not. That's not changing."

"And here I had such high hopes that you'd stay away after prison."

"Sorry to disappoint you. But answer me this, what kind

of a man doesn't want his wife to associate with her own family?

"The kind of man who doesn't want his wife associating with criminals. It's unfortunate when they happen to be one and the same."

"Doesn't it get exhausting?"

"What's that, Nina?"

"Running in circles in your tiny box. How heavy is your morality placed way up on those ill-defined shoulders?"

Kent snorted at her. "Sorry I'm not a reckless thrill-chaser like your boyfriend at the DEA."

Nina stiffened. She clutched the wine glass tighter. She hadn't told Cammy about Beck yet. She didn't know how her sister would react—a federal agent mixed up with someone like her. She was afraid it would offend her sister's sense of worldly order.

"I haven't the faintest idea what you're talking about, Kent. I don't have a boyfriend."

Kent snorted. "Right, right sure thing. Guess my PI was wrong."

Nina's cheeks burned with rage. "You had someone follow me?"

Kent shrugged. "You think I'd let a drug dealer around my wife and children if I weren't one hundred percent positive she was cleaned up?"

"I wasn't a drug dealer," Nina said through gritted teeth.

"Trafficker, whatever. I have to say I was surprised to see you cozying up to one of the good guys. I always figured you preferred your men on the other side of the law. I keep trying to figure out your angle."

"Excuse me?"

"C'mon, Nina. Girls like you always have an angle. I considered that he may be dirty."

Nina shook her head and laughed. "I'm not going to take your bait, so you can shove your snark and theories right up your flabby white ass."

The clack of heels shut them both up. Cammy reentered the room with a cheese plate. Her mouth pulled into a tight, plastic smile.

"Here. These are from *Le Meilleur Fromage* down in the village. Francois really knows his pairings."

Nina smiled thinly and shoved a wedge of Brie in her mouth.

"What time will the others arrive?" Kent said, his eyes not peeling away from Nina.

"Any moment," Cammy said.

On cue, the doorbell rang.

THE ENTOURAGE OF STEPFORD WIVES ON THE ARMS OF PLASTIC Ken dolls arrived one after the other until the living room was bursting with various shades of cotton candy and artificial tan.

Nina now stood cornered in the living room like a waylaid animal, clutching her wine and calculating an exit strategy, as two of Cammy's friends grilled her.

"So, you're the infamous Nina?" A blonde woman said through glossy, botoxed lips. The elegant brunette next to her examined Nina as though she were an article at the freak show.

"The one and only. In the flesh," Nina said, forcing a smile.

Nina had quickly learned that in Cammy's neighborhood, gossip was a competitive sport that had been raised to Olympic standard, and most of the women revered it with all their hearts. She could practically see them salivating over who would get the scoop on Cammy's notorious sister first.

"You must have so many exciting stories," the blonde went on. "I heard you went to jail."

She eyed the tattoo on her forearm and Nina caught the flare of her pupils. Maybe she should have opted for long sleeves.

Nina extended it. "Want to take a closer look?"

"Is that, like, a prison tattoo?" The brunette said with timid intrigue.

Nina shot her a foxy smile. "Estonian mafia."

Both women tittered and jumped backward.

"How's everything going, ladies?" Cammy said, interrupting the awkward.

"I was just getting to know your friends. What a lovely crowd," Nina said, not entirely hiding the bite in her tone.

"Yes, your sister is...charming," the blonde woman said.

"Ladies, if you excuse us for a moment, I need to discuss something with my sister."

Nina tried to stifle a smile as her sister pulled her away.

"What are you saying to them?" Cammy said, sounding almost like a scold. Nina heard the echo of their mother.

"I didn't say anything to them. They're the ones who look at me like I'm the freak of the day."

"They just don't know what to make of you," Cammy said with a small smirk. "You intimidate them."

"Just because I don't shop at the same cotton candy vomit store."

Cammy chuckled. "Come on, Nina, don't be such a catty bitch."

"But it's what I'm good at," Nina said.

"They just don't know that much about you. You understand."

"And whose fault is that? You know, you could set the record straight now and again."

Cammy snickered. "And miss the drama? Look, I explained it to them, but come on, see your story from my side. You went to prison for drug dealing and tax evasion after your kingpin boyfriend faked his own death, then the Estonian organized mafia comes after you? How do you really explain something like that to this crowd? It's hardly believable."

Nina blushed and laughed. "Truth is stranger than fiction?"

"I'm just glad you're out of this whole thing, frankly." Cammy tilted the wine bottle into her glass, then Nina's. She met Nina's eyes. "I'm just glad you finally get to live a normal life and be a part of the family again. I know mom's happy about it too."

Nina snorted. "Mom happy about me being back? I highly doubt it. But thanks for saying that, anyway."

Allison Sullivan had pitted her daughters against each other their entire lives. Despite it, Nina had always idolized her big sister. But without intention, Cammy had cast a broad dark shadow over Nina's entire childhood. It had been difficult not to simmer on it in moments of weakness. And Allison only poked the fire at every opportunity.

"She is, Nina, whether she shows it or not. You know how she is. She has trouble expressing herself. But she loves you. She always has."

"Then why doesn't she ever call me? Want to see me?"

Cammy sighed and took a long sip of her wine. She licked a dewy wine droplet from her pink lips. "Because she's afraid of losing you again."

Cammy's words sliced right to the center of her. The admission was right on the tip of her tongue. *I'm going undercover, Cammy. I might die. But I love you.*

But Nina couldn't bring herself to say it. She couldn't bring herself to shatter the new reality that she had created. To throw it all away.

Instead, she leaned in and hugged her sister tightly.

"I really love you, Cammy. Thank you for letting me back into your life. I'm so glad I've gotten to know Abby and Jacob."

Cammy stiffened, then returned the embrace. She pulled away after a moment and Nina thought she might have seen the sheen of tears in her sister's eyes. But the stoic woman that she was, Cammy quickly blinked them away and averted her eyes.

Cammy brushed a lock of hair out of Nina's face. A soft, sisterly gesture.

"Me too, Nina. Just stay out of trouble, okay?"

## 14

---

Dawn broke against the night, its faint light rousing Nina from familiar, fitful dreams. The brisk air teased the curtains through her open window, allowing a wisp of cleansing air to tickle her senses. She shivered slightly, pulling the covers tightly around her, savoring the sensation of her prickled flesh. She took a moment to savor the feel of her own bed beneath her, the smell of her room, the gentle cadence of a mountain morning. The feel of her heart at a steady pace.

She pulled herself up, pulled on a sweatshirt and stepped out onto her small front porch. A smoky dawn fanned across the skyline, bathing the trees and mountains in a steely, violet glow.

The rains had relented and now the air was brisk, cleansed of sins and desires and human destruction. For a few moments, nature was free to bask in its own glory, a pine-blanketed setting of compelling majesty. She sat for a long while watching the morning unfold, witnessing the subtle rustle of leaves and small animals either retiring their nocturnal pursuits or just getting started on their daily routine.

A tightness snaked through her chest as she thought about holing herself up in that casino. About putting her life in the hands of monsters. Monsters who would not stop to witness the dawn.

The past week had been grueling with nonstop prep work and planning for Nina's descent into the underworld. A world in which she never thought she'd find herself again. She assigned duties of the restaurant to Reina, faking an illness to keep her out of sight. Whether Reina was buying her excuse or not, she wasn't letting on.

Nina was confident in the story they'd concocted, delicately weaving together truth and fabrication about the events of the last few months. O'Malley's seemingly youthful naiveté set her on edge, but she had to have faith. He'd survived thus far on the inside and she trusted Beck's judgment.

What she didn't have full confidence in was her ability to play the part anymore. Before, she'd convinced herself so thoroughly that she was The Cat that their identities were one and the same. In no time, she was no longer playing a part. But she had moved past that identity long ago. She'd seen through the darkness and the smoke and found clarity, regaining her humanity and integrity. Now, she had to walk in there and be just as ruthless and uncaring as the rest of them. She wasn't sure she had it in her.

But then, another part of her was deathly afraid of how easily it all might just come back.

It was all still so evident in her memory—the training, the clothes, the look. A delicate balance between elegant, formidable, and deadly. She'd managed to do it better than anyone. She struck fear into people while keeping her lipstick perfect. How good she'd been at it had been part of the high.

NINA SAT IN FRONT OF THE MIRROR. SHE SMUDGED THE eyeliner under her eyes until the green smoldered. She applied a coat of red lipstick. She secured diamonds in her ears and around her neck and fastened the tennis bracelet around her wrist—a gift from Luther in Prague. The cold stones infused her with memory. The weekend in an ancient castle, decadent food, expensive champagne. Dangerous romance. She had ignored the real reason they were there— so that Luther could sign deals with international drug traffickers. She hadn't wanted to think about the consequences back then. Now, it was all she could think about. She'd been told to bring next to nothing, but maybe wearing Luther's diamonds would add to her credibility with Leksik. A sign of her continued loyalty and affection.

She met Beck's eyes in her reflection. She'd seen that look a thousand times before in men. It was the desire to hold her back, to put her in a cage to keep her safe. The kind of possessiveness that comes with a love that doesn't quite understand you.

She didn't blame him. But it didn't change anything. They both had roles to play now.

"I know you're not happy. And I'm sorry," Nina said.

"No, you're not."

Nina shook her head and focused on her reflection.

"Is there something you're not telling me?" Beck said.

Nina snapped around and met his gaze—the blue smoldering to a smoky gray as they did in times of heightened sensation. "Excuse me? Like what?"

The question worked its way free from his jaw. "Are you working with the organization? Maybe have more going on with Leksik?"

Nina's jaw dropped. The words stunned her. "I'm not even going to justify that with a response."

"That doesn't help."

She guffawed. "Of course not, Beck. That's ridiculous."

He stared at her hard. She saw the pain reflected in the tempest of his eyes.

"I know this is hard, Beck. But you have to be stronger than this," Nina said, hearing the salt in her tone. She was good at lashing out to create distance when she got too close, became too vulnerable.

Beck smirked and didn't take the bait. "You mistake strength for recklessness. Being strong is recognizing the danger and going in anyway. This isn't about being strong."

"Stop. You being angry about the situation doesn't help anything."

"I can't help how I feel. You're putting yourself at risk needlessly."

"You get your opportunity to go in nobly, guns blazing, and be the hero. I just want to do my part."

"You don't have to atone forever, you know."

Nina looked up and met his steely eyes. "Don't I? I think some mistakes require a lifetime of atonement."

He grabbed her hand. "Nina please. Think about your safety. Think about us."

"I am. Because without our integrity, we're nothing, Beck. All it takes for evil to triumph..."

"Yeah, I know."

"Last I checked, I think we're the good guys. At least I really want to be."

Beck's eyes ran over her. He gently touched the two-carat diamonds on her ear, then fingered the matching necklace.

"Where did you get all this?" he said.

"It's from...before."

"Evidence of your past crimes?" Beck cocked his eyebrow.

Nina smiled softly. "One doesn't toss diamonds aside, even if they were bought with blood money."

Beck pressed his lips into a tight smile. "You look good."

"Good?" Nina said, raising her brow.

"Okay, you look stunningly beautiful. I just don't really want to admit it."

"Not one for compliments?"

"Not when it's all for the benefit of someone else."

Nina turned her attention back to the mirror. Yes, it was still her, the same eyes, the same angle to her face. It was like the Showtime version of herself, painted and glittered. A peacock ready for display. Gone was the rough-and-tumble leather, the ripped cuticles and the oven burns that had been her persona these past couple of years. These people were vipers with sharp fangs, devouring their prey without a second thought. Nina had to make herself into that. She shuddered and turned away from the mirror.

Sometimes you just can't look in the mirror. It will strangle your will to survive.

"You know this is all a game, right? It's just a role, a part. Nothing I say to Leksik in there means anything," Nina said.

"I'll try to remember that."

Nina laughed. "You have a flair for the dramatic, you know that Beck? I'm starting to think the big tough federal agent has a romantic streak."

"I've been known." He grabbed her then and pulled her close, pressing his mouth to hers hard.

Nina kissed him back, wanting to lose herself in that kiss. Wanting to pretend that she didn't have to enter the lion's den, didn't have to face her fears, her past, her future. Wanting to be lost in that moment with Beck forever.

She allowed herself a few moments before pulling away. She wiped away the smudged lipstick on his mouth. "There's no room for sentiment here. There's no room for weak emotion."

She turned back to the mirror and touched up her lips.

"Is that how you see emotion? A weakness?" Beck said.

"No, but Luther did. Leksik will. If I'm going to do this right I have to get into character."

Beck laughed.

"What's so funny?"

"How we turn each other into the people we swore we'd never be. Vulnerable. It's the reason so many agents don't have families or loved ones. Easy targets."

Nina understood that all too well. There was some truth that back in her days with the organization she had distanced herself from her family on purpose. As though deep down, part of her knew she would put them in danger.

"What are you going to do about the restaurant?" Beck asked.

"I can leave it in Reina's hands until I...until I get out."

Get out. It was like she was going to prison all over again. And the possibility that she might not make it out alive was all too real.

Toulouse purred, twining around her feet.

"And this guy?" Beck reached down and stroked the cat's neck. Toulouse nuzzled into his palm.

"Feed him for me?" Nina choked back a sob.

Beck gave a weak smile and stood.

"Sure. Just don't lose yourself in there, okay?" Beck said.

"I survived prison."

"This is different. This is you going back to the thing that broke you."

"It didn't break me. I'm very flexible."

Beck smirked. "I've noticed. Just promise it won't change you."

"Change me how?"

"When you go back there, you'll be surrounded by your old world. A world that seduced you to a dark place. You've come so far since then. Just promise me you won't go back there."

"I promise."

"This whole thing makes me sick," Beck said.

"Join the club. There's nothing we can do about it. You and I chose dangerous professions. We have to live with that."

"I just wish there was another way."

"There is no other way."

"They could kill you."

"I know. But you could die at any moment, too. We both have to live with the risk of death every single day. Because that's the life we've chosen. And I'm okay with that now. I've made my peace."

"I need to tell you, Nina. Before you go in. That I—"

Nina held her hand to his lips. "No. Don't. Tell me on the other side."

Nina checked the time on her phone. She met Beck's longing gaze.

"It's time."

## 15

It was two miles from Tahoe Village to the Nevada state line where the casinos sprang up from the mountains. Nina sat in the back of the cab and watched the blocks roll by with painful slowness. Tahoe Village quickly faded into mountain roads, then another outpost of liquor stores and gas stations, the final stop before entering no man's land.

The low hum of Patsy Cline sang out in a gentle twang from the radio. The Middle-Eastern driver sang along in broken English, delightfully drawling out his vowels. It was almost enough to bring a smile to Nina's frozen face.

The Royale Luxury Casino and Resort rose from the lakeside forest like an oasis, glimmering like a tower of diamonds at the base of the Humboldt-Toiyabe National Forest. It was the first billion-dollar resort casino built on the North Shore and that meant luxury adjacent to hundreds of miles of open space without sacrificing vibe. It also meant a world-class spa, a thumping pool scene in the summer, swanky bars, and a gambling floor as hip as any Las Vegas resort.

It had been a long time since Nina had stepped foot inside any casino, and she wasn't sure what to expect. The places disgusted her. Cesspools of human decay masked as hedonism. No one left a casino better than when they entered. Whether there to gamble, to gorge, to party, everyone left a broken version of themselves. Nina clenched her muscles and held tight to her own constitution. Would she slither into her old life, the energy and vibe of the place renewing her as it once did? How long would it take to break her?

The Royale Casino was a land without memory, the kind of place people went after a divorce, bankruptcy, prison. A final destination for those searching for a second chance at life. Even at nine in the morning, the hum of hope buzzed on every side of her; people dreaming, worrying, planning, thinking. Sensations assaulted her on every side—the jingle of slots, the glittering lights, the laughter, the smell of liquor and perfume and lies.

She kept her spine straight and her chin up as she put one high heel in front of the other. It had been a long time since she'd dressed up like this. A long time since she didn't just throw on boots, jeans and a T-shirt, covered in grease and beer. She couldn't remember the last time she'd tanned her legs and slipped on stilettos.

She walked past a massive sports book—that part of the casino where hopefuls wager on professional sports from football to horses—where huge crowds sat tailgating-style in front of floor-to-ceiling screens, cheering and jeering as though they were live. It was enough to make Nina roll her eyes.

Casinos were mathematically designed to separate people from their money. Every bet made in a casino was calibrated within a fraction of its life to maximize profit while still giving players the illusion that they had a chance. Casinos meant cash. And Nina knew that there was no type of business in the world where as much paper money was handled on a daily basis, making it ripe for laundering.

Faint fear spread through her chest as she moved deeper into the lair—partially afraid that she was bidding the daylight farewell for the foreseeable future. In truth, she knew very little about Leksik Vahtra. Would he be just like Luther, just older and wiser? More sinister? His face lingered in her mind like something out of the tail end of a dream—more essence than shape.

Finally, without realizing it, she reached the designated meeting point by the elevators.

A massive man in a suit waited, large hands folded, staring her down with expectation.

"Ms. Sullivan?" He said, his tone carrying the sharp tick of Russian.

"Yes. You are?"

He said nothing. Nina cocked her hip and narrowed her gaze, waiting.

Finally, he spoke. "Yegor. Mr. Vahtra has been expecting you. Follow me, please."

Without waiting for a response from Nina he turned and walked through the casino. Nina took one glance behind her and followed, feeling like she was walking past the point of no return.

They snaked through the central part of the casino, then into the hotel. The man scanned a keycard on the door, leading them into an ornately decorated hallway. Without warning, he shoved her against the wall.

"Hey, what the hell?" Nina said. Yegor's massive hands held her in place as he frisked her for weapons. Finding nothing, he stepped back. He yanked away her purse and rummaged through it.

"Must be sure," he said. He pulled out her cell phone.

"You can't take that."

"No phones." Yegor slipped it into his coat pocket.

Nina rolled her eyes and straightened herself, but she wasn't surprised. In fact, she'd planned for it.

Yegor led her down the hall, then through another door into an alcove with a private elevator. He pressed the button and they waited. It felt like an eternity until the doors finally opened and revealed an opulent carriage, its Baroque design in sharp contrast to the modern luxury of the rest of the casino.

The elevator ascended one painstaking floor at a time, the seconds ticking by slow as winter molasses. Finally, it dinged an alert at their intended destination—the penthouse. They stepped out into another long hallway with only a scattering of doors. The man led her to one at the end of the hall where two additional men in matching dark suits stood sentry.

They stared at her, assessing her. Their eyes darted down her figure, not lecherously but inquisitively. They were sizing her up, evaluating if she had it in her to do what would come next, perhaps.

Nina thrust back her shoulders and met their eyes directly. Without words she told them all that yes, she was ready, she was prepared. Now take me to him.

Yegor nodded at them with finality and opened the door.

Nina breathed one last time and stepped through. The door was like the sound of a tomb closing behind her.

$\sim$

THE ROOM SMELLED OF SPICE AND MUSK AND EXOTIC PLACES. Foreign lands, rich foods. Sex and desire and life.

His energy engulfed her before she laid eyes on him. There, in the corner of the room in a plush leather chair, sat Leksik Vahtra.

She stood at the mouth of his lair, waiting, thinking, breathing.

Finally, he looked up and acknowledged her. His lips spread into something like a smile.

"Nina. Come in."

Nina summoned all the courage she could muster from the pit of her stomach and walked toward the man who would decide her fate.

She stopped in front of him. He didn't get up. He wore a sharp charcoal gray suit, with a slight sheen to its texture that showed off a well-defined physique. His dark eyes smiled, the creases encasing them hinting at his age. But with sharp, angular features, he was still handsome, still vibrant.

He looked like he'd seen and done things. War. Foreign skies. A man of the sea and wild places. Yet there was something beneath his powerful exterior that seemed somehow . . . Fractured. He looked like the kind of man who was more likely to stare a confession out of someone than beat it out of him.

"Hello, Leksik," Nina said. "It's nice to see you again after all this time."

She tried to keep her tone steady and calm, poised, in control. Her heels threatened to wobble, and she clenched her stomach muscles to stay steady.

"It's vonderful to have you here," Leksik said, his accent sharp, seductive. "Yegor, has she been searched?"

"She's clean."

"Good, good.

"He took my phone," Nina said.

Leksik nodded in understanding. "Yes, it was necessary. I will provide you with a new one. Now, please sit. Let me get you something to drink."

"Thank you." Nina said, gently, carefully sitting in the chair across from Leksik.

Leksik snapped his fingers to a woman standing in the corner and within a moment she brought a tray with two glasses of ice and a shaker. With one deft hand, she shook the shaker vigorously, then poured the crisp, clear liquid into the two glasses.

"Thank you," Nina said, accepting the drink but not making eye contact with the server.

She took a slow sip, trying not to down it in one drink. The crisp and cold floral taste attacked her senses.

"We will have much to discuss, but why don't we take a few moments to relax and catch up?"

"Yes, we have much to discuss. What brings you to Lake Tahoe?" Nina said.

Leksik snickered. "Such small talk. Yet you make it sound as though it is important."

Nina smiled and tilted her head. She tried to summon seduction, enchantment, an air of mystery, but she doubted Leksik would be easily fooled by even her most perfected charms.

"I shall leave the direction of the conversation in your hands then," Nina said.

Leksik sipped his own drink, set it down, then sat up straighter. Each movement was deliberate, relaxed.

"Yegor, please clear the room."

Yegor hesitated. He glanced at Nina warily. "*Ser—*"

Leksik flicked up a hand. "I'm perfectly capable of taking

care of myself around this fine young woman. I know her reputation precedes her, but she is not so rude as to hurt her host after they have shared a drink, is she now?"

Leksik looked to Nina with eyes that could peel flesh from bone.

She smiled easily. "You're perfectly safe with me, Mr. Vahtra."

Yegor did not look pleased, but he obeyed and ushered everyone out.

Leksik waited for a beat before speaking.

"I came to Lake Tahoe because I have a great interest in the business going on. As you know, Luther was my man here in Tahoe. He oversaw everything and now he is no longer in a position to do so. So, I needed to step in and take a more hands-on approach. I'm afraid I don't quite have someone here on the ground I can trust the way I trusted my dear nephew."

The thought of Luther came over her and her body shook. She wanted to ask. She wanted to know what had become of him. Did they know? Where was he? But she dared not let on that she knew anything. If anyone asked her, Luther was dead.

"I was pleased you agreed to come work with us," Leksik continued.

"It was an offer I couldn't refuse. Besides, there's nothing left for me out there anymore. It's all so...pointless."

Leksik nodded thoughtfully. "Out there, you have a black mark. Here, you will be revered for your sacrifice. I want to know what happened between you and my nephew."

Nina's pulse thrummed. "What happened?"

"Yes. What happened six years ago. What happened a few months ago. I want to understand the full picture."

"I..." Nina swallowed hard. "I thought he was dead. For a long time. Everyone did. You can imagine how relieved and surprised I was to see him alive a few months ago."

"But you had moved on?"

"I had to."

"The organization would have had you back."

Nina forced her eyes to water. "I was in a state of too much grief. Too much had happened. After prison, I just needed the quiet. I'm sure you can understand that."

Leksik smiled—a neutral smile that revealed nothing.

"And when Luther returned, you went to him willingly?"

Nina blinked innocently. "But of course. We were going to start over. The Feds were on my tail. We had to leave to be safe. But—" Nina wiped a forced tear. "But they caught us before we could get away. And they—well, I'm told they shot him."

"Is that what happened?"

"Yes, I...I was in the lake house cabin. Waiting for him to return. And then..." she shook her head.

"But they found one of his Capos dead. Throat slit."

She could still smell the blood. Feel the flesh give way. "Yes. Well, he tried to rape me. No one gets away with that."

Something like desire stirred in Leksik's eyes. "No one could fault you."

"I suppose Luther and I were always star-crossed," Nina said.

Leksik gave a faraway look that said he might understand a star-crossed romance. "Some people are like magnets to each other. They are both powerful forces, destined to draw the other in. But some people like this should never meet. The fallout spreads too wide, taking out too much."

"You can't always control that though, can you?"

Nina said.

"No, one cannot control this thing. And we do not always know this about the person that we meet. You and my nephew were such people. You were destined to destroy each other. It was no fault of your own. You were built from the same things of this earth. Forged in the same fires at the pit of the universe, cast across the world from one another and somehow, your souls found each other against all odds. The universe tried to keep you apart, I think. But the bond was too strong."

"You sound a bit mystical, Leksik. I didn't take you for a fan of divination."

"That is the problem with the west. You have forgotten about the stars. Forgotten that there are things at work in this universe bigger than you."

"Lots of people have religion," Nina said.

"Religion is simply a set of rules intended to control populations. I'm talking about the great power of the universe."

A long moment of silence stretched out before Leksik sighed and went on.

"For what it's worth, I believe you. But I want to know more about you."

"I would assume you had a file six inches deep on me." She pressed her drink to her lips to hide her nerves.

"My nephew did not speak of you in detail. I knew vaguely what your role was, many years ago. But we're far from those days, no? So, tell me, what have you been doing these past years? Where have your claws been?"

"Just trying to rebuild my life."

Leksik remained silent, his liquid black eyes studying her.

Nina tried not to squirm.

"You've done very well for yourself. A home, a business."

"I've been known to land on my feet."

"A cat indeed." A sly smile spread across his sharp jawline. "I hope that you will find your accommodations here most comfortable. I've set you up in one of our finest suites, just down the way for me. Anything that you want, you need? Just ask. You will have security and service at your disposal twenty-four hours a day."

Impressive, but Nina knew better than to take gifts like that at face value. This was not a vacation. "That's very generous of you," Nina said, trying to hide her nerves. "I'm sure I'll be very comfortable."

"Yegor will show you to your room so you can rest up. We have a lot of business to attend to, you and I."

Nina's executive suite at the Royale was nothing short of luxurious, ornately appointed with antiqued grandeur. The room smelled of musk and cinnamon, amber and vanilla. Sensual and alive. She found the bathroom well-appointed with luxe toiletries, hair styling tools, and a plush robe.

She walked to the walk-in closet and gasped to find a neat row of sleek black dresses hanging. She checked the tags and balked at both the Prada labels and at the fact that they were her exact size.

Not surprising, a number of pairs of sleek heels—also in her size—sat below.

Nina sat on the bed, taking in the scene, and realized that Leksik had no intention of letting her leave the casino any time soon.

She had just walked into a luxe prison cell.

## 16

Nina lay on the bed, staring at the ceiling, but she was too rattled to rest. She needed to walk, to clear her head.

She headed down to the casino, certain that her every move was being monitored, but not caring.

Her entire body trembled with overwhelming anxiety and exhaustion. She wandered the halls of the casino, aimlessly searching for distraction. Gutter-mouthed bachelorettes screeched. Hopeful frat boys eyed them hungrily. Elderly men with desperate eyes clung to their last quarters as they debated slipping them into the slots for one last shot at freedom.

Freedom. The one thing she'd always craved and now Leksik was offering it to her. But even if she'd been inclined to take it, it was all an illusion. She would never be free. A deal with the devil always costs you your soul.

She spotted Agent Shay O'Malley strolling the floor out the corner of her eye. His dress was expensive but youthful—trendy, complicated jeans and a quasi-Western button-down shirt. He caught her eye and made a beeline for her.

"Nina," he said in sort of a whispered shout.

She kept walking, picking up the pace. Damn him, he was being far too obvious.

"Shh," she whispered. "What is it?"

"I have your supplies," he said. "And I need to talk to you. Can we sit somewhere?"

Nina glanced around subtly, checking for eyes on them, and gave a curt nod. "Go to the poker bar top down at the end. It's where the low rollers hang out. There won't be anyone important there."

She and O'Malley slithered into two barstools and she slipped a dollar into the digital poker machine. O'Malley did the same and they each ordered a drink.

"You look absurd," she said.

O'Malley grinned boyishly. "All part of the role. Naïve trust fund kid wants to play with drugs. They underestimate me."

"You play it well."

"Everything you need—VPN, laptop, phone—it's all in a bag in a locker in the spa. Here's the combo." He slid a cocktail napkin to her with six numbers written down. She carefully slipped her hand over it and subtly slid it into her bra. "Be careful. Do *not* get caught. They will very likely routinely search your rooms, so keep it well hidden."

"Thanks. Now get before someone notices you."

O'Malley said under his breath, "There's something else I need to tell you. They brought someone in you need to know about."

"Be more specific, Seamus."

"Rival guy. Son of some other crime family. It's retaliation. Sounds like this other family crossed Leksik big time."

The base of her spine tingled. She shrugged it off. "So? What do you want me to do about it?"

"I don't know, nothing I guess. Just be diligent. I think shit's about to get crazy. There's something big at play. Really big. Leksik is in bed with some serious motherfuckers."

"Hardly shocking. How do you know any of this?"

"People at the high-roller table talk. I underestimated the caliber of people who'd be in that VIP room. I think we all did."

"I didn't," Nina said dryly. She pressed the DEAL button on the poker machine and sipped her vodka soda. "So, what, you're just telling me this as a warning?"

"Yeah kind of. Just be careful. This is about to turn into a full-on war with retaliations going back and forth. Don't get caught in the middle."

Nina remained stoic, but her stomach turned. She'd been caught in the middle before. She instinctively touched the puckered scar on her neck, courtesy of Luther's enemies

"I appreciate the heads up, but you need to leave now. We can't be seen together."

O'Malley snickered and drained his glass until the ice clinked. "You really are a cat."

"Excuse me?"

"Ungrateful, fickle, false sense of independence."

The anger rushed up her spine, flooding her cheeks.

Nina started as calmly as she could. "I don't know what kind of bush league operation they pulled you out of to be here, but you are in way over your head."

"And I don't know what high-end escort service they found you in, but don't you dare try to tell me how to do my job. You give yourself a little too much credit, honey. You were a drug dealer's girlfriend, nothing more."

Nina laughed incredulously but her cheeks still burned. She didn't blame him for not taking her seriously. She probably wouldn't take herself seriously if she were in his shoes.

Nina took a calming breath and found her balance.

"Look, O'Malley, we're on the same team here, okay? I don't know why we're fighting."

"Because you don't play well with others. And it's going to get you killed."

Nina swallowed the large lump of pride in her throat. "You're right, I do better on my own. But I know we need to work together. I'm sorry for what I said."

He nodded. "Yeah, me too."

"I'm just really nervous about this whole operation. Frankly, I think we're both in over our heads. I don't think Martinez or Beck realizes just how dangerous this is."

"All undercover is dangerous, Nina. I'm not some kid who didn't know what I was getting into. I know I look young and green, but that's by design. Part of my image. I've been in some scary operations before."

"Not like this you haven't."

This time O'Malley laughed incredulously. "Ever been in an L.A. crack den? Ever sat next to somebody shooting heroin up his dick?"

Nina shuddered at the image that it conjured. "Can't say I've had the privilege."

"Ever had someone stick their gun in your mouth and threaten to pull the trigger just to see if you blink?"

"We can play this game all day, O'Malley. We've both seen shit."

"Some more than others."

His self-righteous insolence ripped a nerve. She leaned closer and lowered her tone. "Have you ever been gang raped? Beaten? And then delivered back to your boyfriend so he could beat you some more?"

This time O'Malley's face dropped, and his tone filled with earnest. "I'm sorry that happened to you."

Nina released the tension in her shoulders and shrugged it off. "It doesn't matter. My point is, we've all been through a lot. It's part of the game. Nobody goes into this world on either side expecting to come out without a scratch. So let's just play nice together, okay? Let's not make mistakes and let's get out of this fucking thing alive." Nina stood. "I'm tired and need some rest."

She turned to go but O'Malley grabbed her arm. Their eyes met. "Be careful, okay? Just...watch yourself."

She nodded and pulled her arm away. But his cryptic warning echoed in her mind.

She slipped back into her room, the luxury of it welcoming her like a familiar embrace. She eased into the plush bed, falling into the pillows like clouds. Her body throbbed with stress and adrenaline. She eyed the faux antique telephone on the nightstand. Maybe she needed a little something to help her sleep.

She picked up the receiver and a voice instantly chirped through.

"Miss Sullivan. What can we do for you?"

"Oh, yes, um, I'd like to order a drink please."

"Very good. Of course. Do you have a specific libation in mind? Or would you like the Maître 'd recommendation?"

"Something relaxing, please."

"May I suggest the lavender martini?"

Nina nearly laughed. "That would be perfect."

"Right away, Miss."

The knock came within fifteen minutes. A server entered with a silver tray carrying a single cocktail glass and a chilled shaker. He smiled curiously, then with one swift hand, prepared the drink, poured and set it by the bed.

"Anything else, Miss?"

"Oh, let me see what I have—" Nina reached to find a few dollars in her purse, but the server held up his hand.

"That's not necessary. Mr. Vahtra has taken care of everything." He smiled, nodded and left.

Nina sat back on the bed and lifted the martini to her lips—a faded purple like the wisp of a winter dawn. Its floral effervescence blossomed into her senses. She closed her eyes and relished the small decadence of the moment.

Yes, let the seduction of her soul begin.

## 17

**B**eck knew the Drug Enforcement Administration didn't have the greatest reputation on the street. He blamed the media. They were the uptight hall monitors, following all the rules, perpetually forcing doctors to pay $700 for a DEA license to prescribe lifesaving drugs. Or they were inexplicably hostile jerks trying to keep John Cusack from helping Nicolas Cage safely land a plane full of convicts so he could make it home to his daughter.

Beck didn't care. They were in a constant war—often utilizing unpopular tactics to get the job done. In an effort to infiltrate the dark world of trafficking, they had to be willing to table all self-preservation, all rational state of mind. In Beck's humble opinion, anyone who joined up had to have a few screws loose. He didn't exclude himself from this assessment.

Anyone in law enforcement who'd been undercover knew there was nothing in the world quite like the day before one goes into a job. Beck likened it to astronauts on countdown, parachute regiments lining up for the jump. Suddenly, the world is illuminated through a new, dazzling diamond spectrum, every passing face steals your breath with its beauty simply because it's alive. The mind is crystal clear, alert to every second. Things that have baffled you for months suddenly make perfect sense. You could drink all day and be stone-cold sober. Cryptic crosswords are easy as a child's puzzle.

That final day lasts a lifetime.

The first time he went under, he was just an idealistic, overly-testosteroned kid, still carrying around the ghosts and burden of Jack's death—of his past mistakes. Part of this made him the ideal candidate because he was ambitious, unafraid, and had nothing to lose. But he was also reckless and blind.

The first time he'd stepped into that crack house, it had nearly knocked him flat. They were supposed to be people, but they were nothing but shells of their former humanity. The smell of despair infested the room. A young woman lay on a dirty mattress in the corner. She was in a crumpled ball, her dress torn. Bruises decorated her face and arms, and her hair and thighs were caked in blood.

Bile had crept up his throat. Anger had pulsed through his fists. It had taken every fiber in his body to not react. To play it cool. The men on the scene, whether by choice or by circumstance, were soulless, callous, nothing more than animalistic machines, completely void of all humanity. They treated others like disposable objects. The world had shown no compassion to them—so what did they owe the world?

Beck closed his eyes against the onslaught of images. He counted to ten. He bit his tongue and tried to shake them from his consciousness.

He pulled out the case file on the Opik crime operations and flipped through the contents. It was hard stuff to read about. These guys were brutal, ruthless, lawless. Drugs, arms, people—all just commodities.

He read the latest report.

*A National Security Council report on transnational criminal organized crime released Monday, named Eastern organized crime as a strategic threat to Americans and U.S. interests abroad, representing a significant threat to economic growth and democratic institutions.*

*Newly rising branches of organized crime syndicates and criminally linked oligarchs may attempt to collude with state or state-allied actors to undermine competition in strategic markets like natural gas, oil, aluminum, and precious metals, the National Security Council attests. At the same time, transnational criminal networks in Estonia are establishing new ties to global drug trafficking networks to raise quick capital.*

Beck needed to understand more about Leksik Vahtra. The facts he could read about: He'd been at the head of the Opik crime family since 2003 when his predecessor—his former KGB father—was finally snagged on a 45-count racketeering and laundering indictment crossing international lines.

Leksik, for all his known associations, had never been charged with anything.

The Estonian government was cracking down, with stricter monitoring of borders and increased sting operations to break up both human and drug trafficking rings. But these guys had learned to operate undetected under Soviet rule. They were savvy, sharp, intelligent. They kept operations tight, kept the violence to a minimum. One almost had to admire them.

"What's wrong with you?"

Beck looked up to see Martinez. "Hmm?"

"You've got a constipated look on your face. Didn't get your Cheerios this morning?"

"Does anyone still eat Cheerios?"

"Hardly the point. What's going on?" Martinez took a seat.

"Just reviewing the report. Wondering how the fuck we're supposed to take down a guy who's eluded the Estonian government for fifteen years."

Martinez folded his arms over his chest and sighed. He was looking weary, burdened. Beck wasn't the only one not getting any sleep.

"Well, they didn't have Nina Sullivan in their arsenal, did they?"

Beck tried to laugh, but the idea of Nina being used as a weapon stunted his capacity for humor.

He knew Nina would do things that compromised the very fibers of herself, both for her own survival and the survival of the case. Beck was trying to come to terms with it, but various nefarious scenarios kept dancing through his mind. Would she put on a slinky dress and hang all over powerful men? Would she sleep with them? Would she bear witness to crimes, to murder? Would she be asked to commit crimes of her own?

"Graham, hello? What's with you this morning?"

"Nothing, why?"

"Because you're being a moody shit."

"Do I have to be Miss Mary fucking sunshine every day? Since when am I not allowed to just have a bad day?"

"You're also a terrible liar. You'd think somebody who spent so much time undercover would be able to throw out a bullshit excuse every now and again without sounding like it was completely contrived."

Beck stared out the window. The sun blazed, casting a

golden glow across the distant mountains and the evergreen trees tickling the window. A hawk flew by, landing on a branch. It all felt cold, empty. "Just have a lot on my mind, okay?"

"Can't stomach Nina going in." It wasn't a question, but a statement.

Beck didn't bother arguing. Martinez read him like a book.

"Can you blame me?"

Martinez snorted a laugh. "I will pretend that that's a rhetorical question. Because yes, of course I blame you. I blame you for putting your dick on autopilot."

Beck glared. "You know it wasn't like that."

"Graham, I really don't give a shit what it was like. There's a reason we don't get personally involved with assets and informants. You know this."

Beck opened his mouth to argue but Martinez held up his hand.

"Your excuses don't matter. What's done is done. And now you're all wrapped up in her and there's nothing I can do about it. Other than tell you that you made a huge mistake."

A mistake. Was it? Some days, he wasn't sure.

"Look, Beck. You gotta keep it together okay? You can't let your feelings cloud your judgment."

"So you've said."

"Well, it doesn't seem to be sinking in. You're about this close from getting your ass pulled from this case, understand?" He pinched his fingers together in the air. "I've been covering for you but you're going to blow it. If word about you and Nina goes over my head, shit's gonna fly. You have to curb this hot-headed, protective crap and focus."

Beck nodded curtly. "I'm sorry. I'll do better." He felt suddenly small, like a child being reprimanded.

Martinez sighed and gave Beck a pitying look. "I get that sometimes we get inconvenient feelings we can't control. I'm not a robot. I've got a wife, kids. But right now, Nina's just an undercover asset. A valuable one, I'll give you that, but we treat her no differently than any other asset."

"Can we just talk about the case?" Beck said. His head throbbed. He needed more coffee. He needed a workout. He needed fucking sleep.

"Couldn't agree more."

"I've been reading up on Vahtra. He's one dangerous bastard," Beck said.

"Dangerous is a mild term. I've been in contact with the Estonian consulate. From what they tell me, the man is ruthless. But he's deliberate. He's never reckless. He and his people have a quiet calm about them. They don't go in, guns blazing. These aren't cowboys, these are calculating psychopaths. And that's how he's managed to stay out of prison. So, let's set expectations. What do we realistically think Nina is going to get out of him?"

Beck rubbed his jaw. "Presumably, if she can get close enough to him, he might confide a couple of key things. Hopefully, the path they're using to get the goods up the state. If we can't break the pipeline, we'll never stop the flow, even if we take Vahtra down. We have to hope her relationship with Luther Kavka and the organization gives her instant security clearance."

Martinez pulled out a file and slid it toward Beck. "I want you to study up on this guy."

Beck picked it up and examine the file. Aaron Feinstein. President and CEO of Cerberus LTD.

Martinez continued. "I'm guessing that the Opik family actually owns the casino. Or at least, they're the ones pulling the strings behind the curtain. If I had to place my bet on the table, I'd say Feinstein is the guy Leksik has laundering. If Nina can get access to the books, we might be able to prove the laundering. It won't stop the pipeline, but if there's no way to clean the money, it'll put a serious kink in their operations. And if we can bust this Feinstein, I'll bet good money he'll turn."

"I don't know. I'm not sure we're getting anyone to roll on the Estonians. Those guys flay people alive." Beck flipped through the file. "You really think the president of the company would be this involved?"

"The guy's got a pretty solid finance background. Worked his way up on Wall Street, got into real estate, and then into gaming. From what I understand, he's an arrogant bastard, self-righteous. But he covers his tracks meticulously, controls everything. I'd say he's involved."

Beck folded the folder and put it in his briefcase. "Okay, I'll do some digging." He stood to go.

"Graham, one more thing. You have to promise me you're not going to contact Nina."

Beck shifted, his body going rigid. He didn't say anything.

"I mean it, agent. If you care about her, you won't try. Because that will put her in danger. You need to take all these feelings you have and bury them real deep, okay?"

Beck nodded curtly.

"I want to hear you fucking say it, Graham."

Beck closed his eyes and nodded again. Then he met Martinez with his dark inky stare.

"I won't contact her, sir. She's just another asset. No special treatment."

"Good. Now get out of here and go do your job. Andrei Stepanov is in interrogation one."

B<small>ECK</small>  <small>COLLECTED</small>  <small>HIMSELF</small>  <small>AND</small>  <small>PREPARED</small>  <small>TO</small>  <small>GO</small>  <small>INTO</small> interrogation. He needed to be on his game with this one. Stepanov wasn't a big player, but he was high enough on the ladder that he might be able to lead them to some vital information.

He walked through the station and cringed when he saw Shelley, the office manager, perk up at his approach. He'd tried to avoid her since that desperately awkward night he'd accidentally ended up in her floral sheets.

"Hey, Beck," Shelley said, her round cheeks blushing. She toyed with a lock of platinum hair.

He smiled thinly. "Hey, Shelley."

She'd backed off a little since he'd insisted he wasn't interested in more, but she'd made it clear that her offer was on the table at any moment. He need only whistle.

Beck pitied her a little. She was a nice person, but girls like Shelley were still naive and hopeful enough to think a perceived hero like Beck would sweep her off her feet and into a faraway land. He wanted to sit her down and set the record straight. Women should have affairs with men like Beck, not relationships. If they knew what was good for them, they'd run off and marry an orthodontist.

Men like Beck could only bring repeated heartbreak. Just ask his ex, Debbie. Just ask Nina.

Andrei Stepanov sat in the interrogation room, one hand cuffed to the table.

Beck cracked his neck and began.

"Mr. Stepanov. Nice to see you again. Ready for that chat?"

Andrei spat on the floor.

"I see you got a head start on your criminal career at a young age," Beck said, looking Andrei's file over dramatically. But Andrei wasn't a stranger to the law and he wouldn't be easily rattled.

"You don't know that," Andrei said with disdain. "Those records are sealed."

Beck laughed. "You'd like to think that, wouldn't you? Not where you're from, they aren't. Just took a quick call to get them faxed over. Let's see. First arrest at fourteen for burglary."

"Charges never stuck." Andrei sat back, self-satisfied.

"Dropped to a petty larceny case, I see." Beck ignored him and went on. "By eighteen, you were supposedly a capo for Luther Kavka. But then...hmm, you ended up back dealing like a nobody. What happened?"

Andrei's face contorted, and Beck knew he'd struck a nerve.

Andrei shrugged. "Misunderstanding."

Beck flipped the pages. "Ooh, drug bust. Too bad. Guess they lost faith in you. I didn't know Luther well, but he struck me as the type with very little patience for incompetence."

Andrei turned and glared. "You don't know shit, agent."

Beck closed the file and sat across from Andrei.

"Tell me what you know about Leksik Vahtra."

A flicker of fear flashed in Andrei's pale blue eyes, then he smirked.

"I decline to answer on the grounds that my answer may tend to incriminate me."

"You're not under oath or under arrest. Yet. Why don't you cooperate and make both of our lives a little easier?"

Andrei leaned in. "You're wasting your time, Agent Graham. Like you said, I'm nobody. I can't tell you anything."

"You can tell me who your supplier is. You have pure stuff. Pharma grade. Not American."

Andrei shrugged but stayed silent.

Beck recalibrated. "We have you on homicide. What happens next is entirely in your hands, Andrei."

"You think I tell you where I buy my supply and it help you take down Leksik Vahtra?" Andrei laughed. "You know how many layers there are between him and me?" He leaned closer. "You. Will. Never. Get. Him."

"We can offer you a pretty deal. C'mon, Andrei, you're facing life. What do you have to lose?"

Andrei laughed lightly. "At least I will be alive. I tell you anything, the Opik flay my skin off. In prison or not. I don't know about you, Agent, but I like my skin attached to my body."

## 18

Night had long crawled across the sky when Nina's room phone rang.

O'Malley had come through, leaving all the necessary gadgets she needed in a Royale logoed suitcase with after-market secret panels installed to hide her contraband. She'd been doing her daily dark net search, this time plugging in the names of Leksik's associates, seeing if anything gained traction. She'd found one possible link—a dealer named Andrei Stepanov, known go-between who'd supposedly been recently arrested when a deal went bad. There was some chatter about how likely he wouldn't survive to see a court date.

Nina's stomach turned over at the sound of the phone ringing.

She hesitantly picked it up.

"Nina," Leksik said before she said anything. "Be so kind as to join me in my suite."

Nina glanced at the clock. "Now? It's nearly 11 p.m."

"Something better to do, Cat?"

She swallowed. "Of course not. I'll be there in a moment."

She hung up and glanced to the closet. She knew he would expect her to dress the part.

But first, she strapped the tiny digital recorder inside her underwear.

Yegor stood by the door of the suite like a statue.

Without a word, he opened the door for her and quickly shut it after. Nerves snaked their way across her skin. She shivered.

Leksik sat at his desk, well-suited, scanning something on a sleek laptop. His eyes darted up when she entered. He had the same sharp Slavic features as Luther, but he was darker, chilling, almost robotic and mechanical, as though oil and circuits ran beneath his flesh in place of blood and tissue.

"Nina, thank you for coming so quickly."

"Of course," Nina said trying to keep her tone light and unconcerned.

"Please sit. A glass of Champagne?"

"I'll take a vodka if you have it."

"But of course. A woman after my own heart."

Leksik snapped his fingers and an attendant who'd been waiting in the wings appeared with two tumblers of ice. He poured from an unmarked decanter, but Nina had no doubt the spirit was more expensive than her restaurant mortgage.

"How are your accommodations? I take it you've had time to rest up and settle in?" Leksik said.

He made it sound like she'd traveled a long journey to be there and not just over the state line.

"Yes, thank you. My rooms are exquisite."

"Good. Good, so glad to hear." Leksik raised his glass and they clinked and sipped. He set his drink down and leaned back, folding his hands neatly in front of him. "I thought perhaps it was time that we discuss some business. That's why you're here, right?"

Nina pressed her lips into a tight smile then tried to relax.

"Yes, naturally."

"I need to understand something, and I hoped you could enlighten me."

Her heart pounded but she nodded.

"I need you to explain what happened with Luther."

Nina's entire body went rigid and cold as though a veil of ice had settled over her skin. "I don't know what you mean. I already told you."

"And now you'll tell me again. You see, when he decided to come back, I had my doubts that it was a good idea. Things were going fine in Estonia. He was running things alone and I had a replacement here in Tahoe. But he insisted it wasn't going well and that he needed to return. I knew at the heart of it he wanted to go back to you, but I did not push it. I have never quite understood his obsession with you, but I let it slide. Having him back here to oversee the new project was beneficial."

Nina tried her best not to drain the vodka. She desperately wanted to ask what had happened to him. She needed to know. Did he live on? Was he dead?

Luther had been more than a lover to her. He'd been a mentor. For all of his faults, for all his evil deeds, he was a man enlightened about the world. He was well read, intelligent, insightful. People had called him a psychopath. Perhaps he was. But Nina thought even psychopaths had some level of capability of connecting with others. He had loved and cared about her in his own way. He taught her to shoot, to fight, to protect herself. She wanted to at least know his fate.

"Why were you at the lake the night Luther was shot?" Leksik said.

Nina swallowed hard. Her voice quavered, and dampness pooled under her arms. "I told you. Luther and I were going to run away. The Yucatan. Possibly go back to Estonia. The DEA was on to me. It wasn't safe to stay in Tahoe."

"And you were there of your own volition?"

Nina blinked. "Yes, of course."

Leksik's dark eyes narrowed, the small creases around them giving credence to his prowess. She would put his age around fifty—he had the wisdom of age in his eyes but a level of persistent rogue handsomeness in his sharp jaw.

"You killed this Badger and got away?" Leksik asked.

She breathed through her nose. She was prepared for this. He would ask her about that night a hundred times to flesh out her story, to catch her in a lie. She had to stay consistent and calm.

She said, "He was a fool to think I didn't bite."

"So many of the men we must deal with in this business are bottom-feeders. You left the lake house after this?"

"I heard sirens. The police had found us. I didn't want to be there when they raided."

Leksik nodded as if this all made perfect sense. As if he believed every word out of her lying mouth. She prayed it was true.

"They interrogated you?"

Interrogated. Not interviewed.

"Yes. But I denied ever being there. They found no evidence to prove otherwise."

"You are better at this than most men I know, Nina. I do understand why Luther had so much faith in you."

"Always underestimating women?" Nina said playfully. She needed to test the limits of their relationship, slowly and carefully.

Leksik smiled. "On the contrary. I think you are the most dangerous of God's creatures."

"Are you a God-fearing man, Leksik?"

"It is not God one must fear, Nina. It is his creations."

Without turning around, Leksik signaled to his associate. Quickly their vodkas were refreshed.

"What does the DEA know?"

Nina tried to quell the panic swelling in her. If Leksik wanted information, he would get it out of her. She swallowed hard and tried to stay calm. She'd been over this a thousand times.

"They know you have a big pipeline going. They still don't know how it operates or how it's coming up the state in such large quantities undetected."

"And what have you told them?"

"Nothing."

"And did you cut a deal before? No bullshit, Nina. The truth."

"No. I didn't roll, and I served my full sentence. They had trouble linking me to much and I had a damn good lawyer. Got me off easy, I suppose."

"Three years is no small thing. I commend you for it. Even if it was in a cushy American jail."

"It could have been worse. I'm grateful."

"Yes, much worse. As it still could be for you. But for what it's worth, I trust what you say. Because had you turned, my nephew would have known. And I believe you would be dead."

Nina's heart fluttered. Yes. She almost was.

"So, we can continue with this mutual trust?" Leksik said.

"Of course. That's why I'm here. You promised me financial freedom. I'm sick of slaving away for other people. I'm ready to retire to some island, far away and never look back on this hell hole."

"If you cooperate and help us complete this project, I think that is a very real future for you, my dear Cat." Leksik pulled out a file and slid it to Nina.

"What's this?"

"Information. Plans. I want you to study it and feed it to the DEA."

Nina slowly opened the file. Transcripts. They had to be forged.

"A red herring?"

Leksik narrowed his eyes. "A what?"

"You know, misleading information."

"Ah. Yes. Exactly. I need resources diverted here," Leksik pressed his finger to the paper forcefully. "While actual business is elsewhere."

Nina closed the file and nodded. "When do you want me to talk to them? They won't believe you've given me information so quickly."

"Say you stole it. They seem to think highly of your skills, do they not?"

"Of course. I'll tell them right away."

"Good. Don't fuck this up."

"But—" Nina hesitated but continued. "When they realize the information is false, they'll instantly know something's up. They'll know it's all fake and they'll want me pulled."

Leksik smiled, chilling in its perfunctory quality. "Don't worry about that, Cat. It's all been accounted for."

Nina's spine tingled. She pressed her lips to her glass, focusing on the ice on her tongue, the floral aroma, the sting on her throat. Anything to keep her breath steady.

There was suddenly a knock at the door, sending Nina jumping from her seat.

"Jumpy kitty," Leksik said. "It's only some acquaintances. We have business to attend."

Momentarily, Yegor escorted three well-heeled men into the suite.

"Thank you, Yegor. Gentlemen, welcome," Leksik said, standing and extending a hand to each.

They stared at Nina suspiciously.

"Who is dis?" One said, his voice throaty, sharply accented.

"This, Olev, is Nina. She was once a very close associate of my nephew, Luther. She has an in with the DEA and is assisting us in ensuring they stay off our trail."

"Why were we not told?" Olev said.

Leksik glared at them. "Since when do I need to run my decisions by you, Olev?"

Olev and his friends didn't answer.

Leksik gestured for them to sit. "Good. Now sit. We have plans to discuss."

The men took their seats and the attendant brought them a bottle of vodka, glasses and ice.

"I don't like being caught off guard, Leksik," Olev said.

Leksik raised his hands in capitulation. "Apologies, gentlemen. But you must understand that her presence here is somewhat secret. I could not compromise it."

"Fine. Explain," Olev said.

"Nina here will feed the DEA information we deem

acceptable. In return, the DEA will keep her abreast of what they know of us. This way, we can turn the tide in our favor, put them off our scent."

"You trust this bitch?" Another man said, the insult as careless as the flick of a hand.

Nina's cheeks burned. She dug her nail into her palm to stay composed.

"Language, Serge. Nina is a trusted associate. Offer her respect," Leksik said.

Serge nodded a quick apology to Nina. She raised her chin.

"And yes, I do trust her. She knows well enough what happens to those who betray us, don't you, Nina?"

Nina forced a weak smile to mask her blind fear.

"So what do they know?" Olev said, looking directly at Nina.

Nina repeated what she'd told Leksik.

The room was thick with silence for a few minutes. Nina prayed they couldn't hear the thrumming of her heart.

"I have already given her misleading information to keep them busy while the pipeline is executed," Leksik said.

"And everything is set for the end of the month?" Olev said.

"We are set, my friend," Leksik said.

The end of the month. Two weeks. Nina breathed. She just needed to survive two more weeks.

THE MEETING STRETCHED INTO THE SMALL HOURS OF THE morning. Nina finally fell into her bed but she couldn't sleep, tossing and turning in a nightmare carnival ride. She couldn't shake the fear, the impending doom hovering just outside her window, begging for entry. *Don't let it in.*

She sat at her computer, going through files, trying to make sense of everything, anything. She'd already transcribed all the digital recordings from their meeting and was now trying to piece them together into a way that made sense. Something was off about it, but she couldn't say just what. If she sent the information to Beck under the pretense that it was real, she might be sending him into a trap. But if she told him it was fake, they might not go in naturally, clueing Leksik to her betrayal.

Her stomach twisted, threatening sick. But there was only one option to maintain the integrity of her cover and the case.

She logged into her VPN, diverted her IP address and then accessed the fake email account she'd created for the operation. She typed out a note.

*Next deal information in the file. Encrypted.*

*Please be careful.*

THERE WAS A KNOCK AT THE DOOR THAT STARTLED HER. SHE slammed her laptop shut and nearly fell out of her seat. She pressed her hand to her heart and forced herself to breathe. She checked the clock. 5 a.m. Jesus, didn't these people ever sleep?

"One minute," she muttered.

Slow and groggy, she pulled herself up and checked the mirror. She threw her hair up into a messy bun and ran a swab of concealer under her eyes. She slipped on a bra under her tank top took five collecting breaths. She slid the laptop and VPN back into the secret suitcase compartment.

She slowly opened the door. The guard assigned to her was standing sentry.

"Yes?" Nina said.

"You have someone here to see you."

"Okay. Send him in."

She stepped back from the door and opened it wider. A moment later, a tall, lithe figure slithered in. Her auburn hair was pulled back in a high, sleek ponytail, its long tendrils tickling the alabaster skin of her bare back. Nina sucked in a breath.

"Katie?" Nina blinked a few times, trying to put two and two together. What was one of her old waitresses doing here at the Royale?

"Hello, Nina," Katie said, her voice clicking with a sharp accent she'd never had before.

She wore a sleek black dress and towering black stilettos. Her eyes were smoky, her lips blood red. Glistening emeralds were fastened in her ears, catching the glint in her piercing blue eyes.

Nina had looked into those eyes a hundred times before but now suddenly there was a foreign depth to them, as though a veil had been lifted. A woman of the sea and wild places. Power. Femininity. Force.

"What are you doing here?" Nina's words felt jumbled and shaky on her lips.

Katie's eyes twinkled with satisfaction. She glanced back to the doorman and gave him a subtle nod. He shut the door.

Katie turned around and faced Nina. Finally, it clicked. Nina laughed, the obviousness of it slapping her across the face.

"You're one of them. You always were."

Katie shrugged, the movement fluid and languid. "This

is true. And you are stupid for not noticing. You know, for being this criminal mastermind, you're not very bright."

"You're right. But I suppose it's a testament to you. You're a marvelous actress."

Katie offered a delicate bow.

"What's your real name, anyway? I doubt it's Katie."

Katie scrunched up her face in disgust.

"I think not. Katja Vahtra," she said with pride.

"Katja." Nina rolled the name on her tongue. How stupid she'd been. "What are you doing here? And what, you were sent into my restaurant to spy on me?"

Katja laughed, airy, careless. "Spy on you? Yes, I suppose that is one way to say it. I was there to keep an eye on you. They had their suspicions about what you were up to. And Luther of course wanted to know everything there was to know about your new life."

"Luther? Luther sent you in there? You work—worked —for him?"

"Yes. Luther wanted somebody you would not suspect to send in to find out about your day-to-day life. Your comings and goings. What you are doing these days. Who you are fucking."

"You bitch," Nina said.

Katja smirked. "What is it you say? Sticks and stones."

"I guess I should be used to betrayal by now."

"Right. You should talk about betrayal. Don't think I will forget what you did to my cousin."

"Your cousin? Who?"

Katja moved into the hotel room and made her way over to the bottle of vodka sitting on the dresser. She lifted the bottle, examined the label, then poured a couple of fingers into a glass, not bothering with ice.

"A little early," Nina said, glancing at the dawn breaking outside her window.

"I'm on my way to bed. Long night." Katja slammed back the vodka. "Luther. He is my cousin."

*Is. Not was.* "Luther...he's dead right?"

Katja met her eyes. "And Leksik is my uncle. Great uncle. Something like that."

Nina didn't push it. "Why are you here?"

Katja sat on the bed and glanced around the room. Her eyes landed on the suitcase next to the desk. Nina instinctively moved between Katja and her things.

"I thought you and I should have a little talk," Katja said.

"I can't imagine we have anything to say to each other. You were spying on me. And here I thought you were just a common thief."

"You were always too shortsighted, too trusting. And you have terrible judgment."

"I don't think you're really in a position to judge anything about me. You don't know me at all."

Katja opened her small black clutch and pulled out a pack of cigarettes and a silver lighter.

"You can't smoke in here," Nina said.

Katja lit the cigarette and took a long thoughtful drag. She met Nina's eyes and exhaled, the smoke billowing out through her glossy red lips, like a smoking gun.

"Leksik seems to think something of you. He certainly put you up in fine accommodations."

"Obviously he trusts me," Nina folded her arms over her chest.

Katja smirked. "He doesn't trust you. He just wants something from you."

"We have an arrangement."

"I'm sure you do. But you should know something, dear

Nina. Leksik does not play games he has not already won. Whatever you think you're going to get from this, rethink it. You've already lost."

"I guess that's my chance to take then. But I appreciate your concern. We women have to look out for each other, right?"

Katja took another long, thoughtful drag from her cigarette. Her tone was haunting as she spoke. "Let me make one thing very clear. I will not let you do to Leksik what you did to Luther."

Nina felt a shiver at the base of her spine, as if an ant had bitten her just above the tailbone.

"And what's that? Gain his trust and respect?"

"Destroy him."

Then it dawned on her. "Are you and Leksik—" she let the thought trail off.

Katja's blue eyes narrowed. "It is none of your business what Leksik and I are. But it is something that you could not possibly understand."

Nina studied her, really studied her. "I think I've heard of you. Luther spoke about a young cousin back in Estonia from his father's side. Said she was a serpent, poisonous. Destined to rain terror on the world. I think that was you."

Katja smiled, a touch too maniacally to instill the sense of ease she'd probably intended it to.

She stood and put her cigarette out on the bedside table.

"Luther was always a smart man but misguided in his love for you. Love makes people so weak. Tell me, have you destroyed your DEA boyfriend as well? Agent Graham, right? Very sexy, I can admit. But clearly stupid."

Nina wanted to argue, but it was futile. Katja would have witnessed enough at the restaurant. She cursed herself for her foolishness.

"I've done what I had to, to earn trust. I'm sure you can understand that," Nina said.

"I don't believe you for a second. You were not faking with him."

"I don't really care what you believe. It has nothing to do with you."

"You should care. Because I will be your downfall, Cat."

"You're nothing but a gopher, doing Leksik's bidding. Or maybe you're just his whore. Either way, you don't scare me."

"You really think you're something, don't you?"

"Maybe you underestimate me," Nina said.

"Says all who are mediocre. You are famous because of your effect on my cousin. Until you, we all assumed Luther was incapable of feeling anything at all. He is a ruthless man, as you well know."

"I know exactly the kind of man Luther is." Nina shuddered just saying his name.

"Do you? Did you know he murdered his own mother when he was just a boy?" Nina's jaw fell. Katja didn't wait for an answer. "But you come along and then all of a sudden, he is different. He seems to care. And he assures us that you are like us. Something powerful. A weapon. And then you put him out, like the butt of a discarded cigarette. You rip out his heart."

Nina laughed incredulously. "You have an interesting version of the truth, Katja. I wasn't the one ripping hearts out. You have no idea what I went through because of him."

Katja looked at her with melodramatic pity. "Poor thing. He hit you? He used your little pussy too hard?"

"I was raped and beaten. Retaliation from Luther's enemies."

Katja waved her hand. "Is that all?" She stepped closer

and stroked the puckered scar on Nina's neck. "You have no idea what might happen to you next. Rape is the least of your concerns."

Nina's stomach turned over, but she lifted her chin. "You don't frighten me, Katja."

Katja tilted her head. "Good. Because someone too stupid to be afraid will be easy to take down."

Nina tried not to show the fear in her expression but staring into Katja's eyes was like staring into the abyss. She saw her own demise unravel in the nightmare of them.

Katja picked up her purse and straightened her spine. In full regalia, she towered over Nina.

"You're just a novelty to them. A thing they do not understand and therefore wish to control, wish to own. But your shine will wear off once they see not everything that glitters is worth something. Watch yourself, Cat. You're on your last life. If you do anything to remotely betray us, I will rip apart your entire family."

With a cunning smile, she left. Nina was sure she saw a forked tongue beneath her red lips.

# PART II

---

*Because the drug war abuses exploited women, they are more likely to be jailed than men. The number of women serving time in prison for drug-related crimes surged by 271 percent through the 1990s and 2000s. It's almost three times the rate of increase for men.*

*- North American Congress on Latin America*

## 19

E very sound echoed off the cold concrete walls of the Royale basement as Nina stood in anticipation.

Katja stood beside her, looking both gothic and elegant in a sleek pantsuit, long pale fingers artfully whisking a cigarette between red lips.

Nina's stomach turned over as she saw the product pulled from the bags. She had certainly seen her fair share of drugs during her time with Luther, but nothing like this. The sheer quantity of it set her teeth on edge. She was no longer naive to the horrors that this small substance would inflict on communities, on families, on nations. She now knew how it would destroy lives, tear people apart, kill people, young children. Kids like Beck's brother who didn't know any better, making stupid decisions out of boredom, depression, or loneliness. Women who got hooked by circumstance. People who, in one moment of weakness, sent their entire existence spiraling out of control.

Women like Brooklyn and Reina.

Women like Melanie.

But in that moment, Nina remained stoic and still, her

spine frozen erect. She tilted her head slightly as though she were examining the product with objective scrutiny. She forced her muscles not to react, forced her eyes not to reveal her true feelings on the matter. She couldn't give Leksik anything other than indifference.

Katja leaned in and whispered in Nina's ear.

"Beautiful, isn't it?"

"I suppose," Nina said. She was getting a headache from keeping her muscles and jaw clenched so tightly.

"When I see this, I laugh at all the stupid people. And I laugh at how I'll spend their money." Katja's voice was sharp, as though it had been whittled to a fine edge on a whetstone.

"Yes, we're going to be very rich from all this. Have you decided on how you're going to spend all those thousands of dollars that Leksik is going to kick your way?"

Katja's sharp eyes narrowed at the insult. She dragged her cigarette and blew the smoke into Nina's face.

Nina refrained from coughing. She wouldn't give her even the slightest satisfaction.

"You think that you are so untouchable. Don't believe I didn't know what happened to you before. I know how you crumbled and caved the moment you were under threat." Katja leaned in and dropped her voice. "I know you have caved again. I know you have a weakness for this DEA agent. And when I can prove that, it will be your downfall. I will use it to destroy you, trust me."

Nina didn't bother looking at Katja.

"Katja, my dear, I don't trust you as far as I can throw you. And forgive me if I don't find your threats to have much weight. You made a terrible spy, after all. I mean, even some two-bit side piece such as myself caught you in the act."

She almost felt Katja's cheeks warm, the heat bouncing off of her.

"We will see who wins in the end."

"Yes. We will see."

"What are you two going on about?" Leksik said. "Stop gossiping and come here."

Katja tossed her cigarette butt to the floor and stubbed it out with the toe of her pointed stiletto.

They stepped up to the now massive heap of bagged pills.

"This, my darlings, is your freedom," Leksik said.

Nina sucked in a breath at the sight of it all. "It's beautiful," she said, the words coming out in a whisper. "Is it...Mexican?"

Leksik snickered. "No. They are helping us get it in the country and up the state, but this is coming from Eastern manufacturing. It's much cleaner. Pharmaceutical grade, equal to anything you'll get here in the states. Our production plants in Estonia are contracted with the Swiss."

Nina swallowed, making mental notes. She had to remember everything. Every detail. Every glance.

Leksik touched her arm lightly. "We have an important client coming in. Nina, I want you to meet with him. Attend a poker game tonight."

She met his dark eyes. "Poker?"

"You don't have to play—although I heard a rumor that you're an accomplished player. I just need you to be present."

"Why?" She tried to keep her tone even and authoritative. Was this a test?

"Because you negotiate well, have a strong presence. And because you're American."

"What does that have to do with anything?" Katja spat the words.

Leksik shrugged. "Creates an immediate level of trust. People like what they know and understand. And American men love a beautiful woman."

The door opened then, and Nina heard the click of heels on the concrete floor.

"Ah. The next order of business," Leksik said.

Women of various shapes and sizes stepped into the room ushered by Yegor, their heads hung low. They were scantily clad but not so much that it suggested they had been recently working the streets. They were clean, but hollow. Mere shells of what might have been vibrant young women in the not too distant past.

Nina could think of only one thing—mules.

Katja watched them with an amused expression. She lit another cigarette.

"Those will kill you, you know," Nina said.

"I will never live that long." Katja brushed past Nina to join Leksik in front of the women.

Leksik examined the newly arrived guests with pleasure, a horseman admiring a new steed. His face assumed the expression of a pilgrim beholding the promised land. Nina's stomach turned.

The young women filed in and obediently lined up against the wall as though it was a familiar drill.

Sometimes it would appear that the best explanations were really just the simplest. Traffickers had been using certain techniques since the eighties. And despite new technology and developments, some ideas and operations were still the best way to go. Human mules.

Nina had always known about mules, but she'd never stood witness to them in action. The truth was, globally, women continued to earn less and had fewer rights. They were easily persuaded into endeavors like this for lack of better options. She'd read the statistics. Women were far more likely to be arrested for their trouble. It was the same conveyor belt of incarceration, with an extra dose of blithe inhumanity for the mothers, sisters, and daughters forced into this life by circumstance. Trafficking abused already exploited women. And there was no one to protect them. Nobody cared.

Nina sucked in a breath when she saw that one of them was near full-term pregnant.

Leksik walked over to the line of women—girls, really. They were so thin and gaunt that it was difficult to tell their ages, but they looked like teenagers to Nina.

Leksik rubbed his jaw as though he were studying them, considering them, like cattle at a stockyard.

"Hello, girls," Leksik said in English. None of them answered him. "I know we've never met directly and you might be wondering why I've called you in person. But that shouldn't be a mystery. I'm very disappointed, I must admit. I am told that one of you lost your cargo."

The girls shifted in place but did not raise their eyes.

Nina's stomach tightened in phantom empathy.

Leksik paced. His sharp features took on a look of sympathy. "I don't think that I ask so much of you, do I? I give you a simple task. I pay you well. But it would seem that that is not enough. You don't take any pride in your work," he went on like a scolding father.

One girl found a sliver of intrepidity, and she raised her eyes. Bright blue orbs, a thin face, almost preternatural, long blonde hair in a low braid.

"*Pozhaluysta*," she said. Nina recognized the Russian word. *Please.*

"English," Leksik said like a schoolmaster.

"Don't hurt zem," she said. Her voice was defeated, resigned.

"Are you admitting that it was you who messed up?" Leksik said.

The girl nodded timidly. "*Da*, it me. I mess up. Don't hurt zem." She glanced to her sisters in arms.

"What happened?" Leksik said.

The girl chewed her lip. "It come out too soon. I has no choice but to get rid of it. Police everywhere."

Leksik smiled, chilling, mechanical. "Why didn't you re-swallow it?"

The girl's doe eyes stretched, looking anime over her gaunt face. "Swallow, after...?" she glanced down at her lower region.

Leksik waved his hand. "Never mind. For your candor, I will not kill you."

The girl visibly exhaled, a wave of relief washing over her.

Leksik looked to the rest of the girls. "The rest of you, go dump your wares. Katja will take you into the back and ensure that everything made it all right. If you have trouble passing, we have your favorite chocolates."

*Dump their wares.* Nina had always known it was part of the trade—mules who carry capsules inside their stomach, bowels, anuses, and vaginas—but she'd never seen it in the flesh. She heard a doctor describe them as ticking time bombs. If a capsule cracked open, the mule's chances of survival were slim.

How could she have been so blind for so long?

"Come. You all stink," Katja said. The girls followed in a neat line as Katja led them to a back room.

Leksik turned his attention back to the woman who had confessed. "What is your name?"

"Misha," she said. Her blue eyes stayed defiantly locked on Leksik's.

Nina wanted to hug her, tell her she was brave. Tell her it was going to be all right.

Leksik grabbed Misha's arm. "Misha. I will allow you to live, but your trespasses do not go unpunished. You will need to suffer your punishment for your stupidity."

Misha raised her chin and nodded. "*Da.*"

Nina's stomach turned as she tried not to imagine what the punishment would be.

Misha's eyes registered her fate, but there was nothing she could do. In a moment, two men had grabbed her and were pulling her out of the room to an unspoken destiny.

Nina closed her eyes, blocking out the images of her own past punishments.

"I can see that this disturbs you," Leksik said, straightening his shirt collar.

Nina wanted to pretend that it didn't, but he would never believe she was so cold and indifferent for it not to bother her.

"Yes. Of course it does. I'm only human, right? But it's just business," she said, the words acidic and ashy on her tongue.

"A lucrative one at that. This helps keep me a wealthy man. And you could be a wealthy woman, Nina. You needn't ever have to worry about the mundane again. Serving bad coffee to ungrateful tourists in some small town—is this really the dream you had for yourself?"

All the pieces of Nina's life flashed before her. Her friends, her new relationship with her family. Beck. The glamour and excitement of her old life. The danger. The death. The horror.

Nina shrugged. "I haven't decided what that dream looks like."

Leksik laughed softly. "Yes, that is what I hear. A woman suffering from sensibilities."

"What will become of her?" Nina looked at the door.

Leksik considered this. "She'll be punished for her carelessness. They know procedure. We trust them with the highest-grade product. And pay them well. And for this, she's too squeamish to do what she must? Besides, there's a chance she stole it anyway. Either way, she knew the risks."

Nina bit her tongue to remind herself she was still human. How much of a choice had these women ever really had?

"And the rest of them? Who are they?" Nina asked.

"They agree to work for us in exchange for a ticket to your promised land."

"Why do you need them if you have other ways to get the product here?"

"Our distribution channels work for the larger quantities, but for the small batch, high-end stuff that will bring in millions? I don't trust that to Mexican pipelines. I want that handled with a personal touch."

A cry rang out from the back room. Misha's eyes flashed in Nina's mind and she swallowed bile.

"Don't look so disgusted, Nina. Given the high-risk nature of transportation duties, they only go on a few runs. Then they can have steady work in the casinos. The ones who prove not so cooperative can assist in other domestic tasks. Housekeeping, service, the like."

"Slaves," Nina muttered before she could stop herself. Her gut tightened.

Leksik snickered. "Slaves. Call it what you like. They had no lives before to speak of. Poverty, starvation. Here they will have good food, a place to sleep. The chance to earn a future. Your entire country was built on this arrangement."

A future? What kind of future would worn-out prostitutes have? Bloomed and faded by the time they were twenty-five, their bodies and minds broken. Nina bit her lip to keep from speaking the vitriol stirring in her mind.

"Where are they from?"

"Why so many questions? They aren't your concern. Not important." He pressed a hand to her lower back. "Come. We have some business, and then we will celebrate with a fine meal and good drink before the game tonight."

Nina spared a glance back to the room where frightened, frail women were taking laxatives to push out balloons of high-grade opioids while Katja watched every move. Nina's whole body shook with the horror of it. She had to find a way to help them. *But really Nina, will you ever make a difference?* If she tried to get involved, to get righteous, she would only compromise what she was there to do and possibly get herself killed in the process. There was a switch she had learned to flick, early on in her days with Luther. It got easier, maybe too easy, with time. One click, somewhere in a corner of her mind, and the whole scene unfolded at a distance, as though on a screen, in living color, while she objectively watched and planned strategies and gave the characters a nudge now and then, alert and absorbed and safe.

She flicked that switch now.

Beck's voice chimed in her ear. *When good men do nothing...*

## 20

**K**atja could not ignore that she had a problem. Every moment that Nina was here in the casino, whispering lies into Leksik's ear was one moment closer to all their demise.

It wasn't jealousy, as Leksik would suggest. She didn't crave romantic fantasies from Leksik, but they met each other's needs. They had a partnership, an understanding. Leksik had no time for fantastical notions of love. Not since Nadia was killed. Katja believed Leksik had been capable of love once. But his wife's brutal death had broken that part of him.

She had never before had to worry that Leksik was going to fall in love with some young thing and make foolish decisions. Katja was the young thing who met his base needs.

But Nina looked far too much like his late wife. And that was not good for anyone involved.

Katja brushed out her red hair and then wound it up into a tight bun. She slipped on a sleek black dress that hugged her frame and slid her feet into snakeskin stilettos. She did not believe femininity was a weakness. Femininity was power, something that men could not tame, could not control. As long as a woman could wield her own femininity, she was untouchable.

People would always underestimate women. Especially women from her background. Poor. Uneducated. Neglected. Sure, there had been great so-called growth in women's rights in Estonia. There was a woman president, after all. But even she was a mere figurehead. The progress, however, did not trickle down to the old families. What the government tells you to do is one thing, what the old-world men of her country would actually do was entirely another. Especially those on the East side, loyal to Russia.

She checked her face in the mirror and reapplied one more layer of red lipstick. Yes, this was enough to do some damage.

Leksik thought Nina was the secret weapon. She would prove she was not some little child.

She went to the small fridge in her room and pulled out a bottle of chilled Perrier-Jouet Belle Epoque champagne. She dexterously popped the cork out and filled a crystal flute. She did not believe in waiting for special occasions to enjoy the finer things in life.

She pressed the flute to her lips and drank deeply, but slowly. She was no longer nervous. The time for nerves had passed. Like love, worry and fear were also pointless emotions. They did not change anything. They only held you back from doing the things that you needed to do. She set down her flute and retrieved her compact Beretta 92 from her desk drawer and slipped it into her handbag.

This wasn't revenge or jealousy, this was righting what was wrong. This was setting things the way they should be. Proving her capabilities.

Her father would have been proud. Her father would

have never sat around, watching the world crumble. He taught her well, served the family well, but he was a maverick, calculating, pragmatic. He had taught Katja to live the same way, not to waste energy on pointless emotions and attachments. It was not the physical pains that would endure, he had told her. It was the psychological ones.

*"Never let them break your mind, Katja. Your body will heal, your mind and heart may not."*

She made her way through the casino, down the plush corridors and finally to the hidden hallway. She scanned her FOB and entered into the world hidden from the idiots below with gilded dreams in their eyes.

He was waiting for her in the lounge, a glass of scotch glowing honey in his hand. His eyes were inky dark, beady. His portly frame tested the fabric of a gaudy suit meant for a man half his size and age.

"Katja," he said. Her name sounded cheap and broken in his crass accent.

"Aaron. Thank you for seeing me."

She didn't actually feel the need to thank him for anything. After all, it was she who would be doing him favors, but he was an arrogant bastard who thrived on feeling wanted and superior.

"Drink?" Aaron Feinstein said. She nodded, and he poured her a few fingers.

"I gotta tell you, Kat, I don't feel good about any of this."

"Katja," she snapped.

"Huh?"

"My name isn't Kat, it's Katja."

"Fine, fine, sorry. Snappy little thing."

"Nobody is forcing you to be here, Aaron. You are the one who thrives on greed."

Aaron shrugged. "Makes the world go 'round."

"It's no secret that I don't like you, Aaron. You're uncouth, fat, and self-absorbed. But you have the connections and clout I need. We have both been overlooked. It's time that I get what was coming to me, and I think you are the man to help me."

Aaron leaned back in her chair and shot her an inquisitive stare.

"What about Leksik, honey? Don't you got some kinda blood bond with him or some shit?"

"I am doing this for Leksik's benefit. He doesn't realize what a mistake he's making."

"You've got some serious balls on you, woman. I'm not sure if you're a fucking idiot or a goddamn genius."

"He will thank me when this is done."

"Or string you up by your entrails."

"I'm not afraid of Leksik. He will not hurt me. He and I are family."

"Yeah, what's up with that incestuous shit anyway? Actually, I don't care. I'll never understand your fucking freak dynamic. It's not really my problem, is it? So, what's my cut?"

Katja shrugged. "Twenty percent."

Aaron roared with laughter. "Try again, little girl."

"Thirty. Don't get greedy, Aaron."

He smirked but nodded. "Thirty will do. Considering you're more likely to get caught than I am."

"You underestimate me. You too will be thanking me very soon."

Aaron reached for the decanter and filled both their glasses. "I just hope you know what you're doing, snake."

"I need you to do something for me," Katja said.

"All ears."

"Get rid of Nina."

Aaron laughed. "Yeah, no. I'm not touching that fucking situation."

"She's a problem."

"You give her too much credit, Katja."

"You give her not enough credit. You cannot underestimate this strange power she seems to have over everyone. Perhaps, my friend, she even has this power over you." Katja arched her eyebrow.

Aaron shifted awkwardly. Powerful women clearly made him uncomfortable. He wiped a bit of sweat from his greasy forehead.

"You worry too much, snake. Nina has nothing to do with anything. Leksik's only using her to get information from the Feds. Once he has what he needs from her, he'll kill her."

"And you're so sure of this?"

"Of course. He has no reason to keep her alive. She knows far too much."

Katja considered this. There was a time in her life when she would've trusted Leksik implicitly. Every word that came out of his mouth was gospel when she was a young girl. But now, she wasn't so sure what was going through his mind.

"I think we should kill her ourselves," she said.

Aaron chuckled. "You're insane. If you go anywhere near that girl, Leksik will have you flayed. Family incest or not."

Katja's glared at him but wouldn't capitulate to the insult.

"Who will tell him it was us? You wouldn't incriminate yourself, would you?"

Aaron threw up his hands. "Hey, I want nothing to do with this. I'm not killing some innocent woman just because she rubs you the wrong way."

Katja snorted. "Innocent? That girl has just as much blood on her hands as anyone."

"Why are you so sure we can't work with her? Maybe she's more of an asset than you think."

"Work with her? She's working with the DEA!"

Aaron remained infuriatingly calm at her outburst. "She's only pretending to."

"Oh Aaron, how much of a buffoon are you, really? She's playing both sides."

"You have zero basis for this. Forgive me if I trust Leksik's judgment over yours. Now, can we get back to actual business here and not your school girl vendetta?"

Katja forced her lips into a smile. "Of course. We have a lot to work out."

As soon as this was done, she'd slit Aaron Feinstein's throat.

## 21

————

After a hearty meal of smoked fish and potatoes, accompanied by full-bodied wine, Leksik and Nina walked through the main floor of the casino.

"The glitz, the glam, the endless buffets and those seas of slot machines. It's all one glittering illusion, to make people believe they're more important than they are," Leksik said. "You see, Nina, the thing that I've learned in my time in business here, is the trick is to make people feel like they are royalty for a day. They leave their shit lives and they come up here with money in their pockets, just ready to toss it in the fire. Women put on their tight dresses, their cheap high heels, while the men loosen their ties and get their wallets handy."

Nina watched the glittering world around them as Leksik spoke. It was a beautiful exposition of hedonism. Human desire. Base needs. Sex, greed, the lust for power. Men like Feinstein and Leksik took these things, packaged them up, then tossed them out like gilded coins and watched the people scramble for their share.

"And yet there is no concern for the detriment to society?" Nina said it more to herself.

Leksik laughed. "You think I should be concerned with these things? Nobody forces these people to be here. Nobody's robbing them of their hard-earned money. They toss it away freely. Nobody's forcing men to cheat on their wives, forcing young women to drink their body weight in cheap liquor and make bad decisions they regret in the morning. This is the human condition, Nina. Welcome to Planet Earth."

It was the same kind of rhetoric Luther used to use when talking about trafficking. It wasn't his fault that people chose to make bad decisions. It wasn't his fault that boys shot up and girls popped pills. If humanity was hell-bent on destroying itself, who was Luther to stand in the way? Humankind had been its own worst enemy since its inception. Luther was just helping it along. In his opinion, the sooner the planet imploded on itself, the better. Then perhaps the Earth could rebuild itself without the plague of humanity. There were days when Nina had to admit that finding goodness was increasingly difficult.

They finally approached the high-rollers' room, guarded by a robotic man in a sharp, three-piece suit. He nodded to Leksik, then opened the doors.

The room was dark, plush, exotic.

It smelled of deceit, betrayal, smoke, and mirrors. All the warning signs Nina knew to trust. But there was nothing she could do but keep her chin up and her senses alert.

She did a quick assessment of everyone. She recognized Olev and his associates. Beside them sat a baby-faced kid who looked barely eighteen. And agent Shay O'Malley smack in the middle. O'Malley shot her a fleeting glance, but he kept his game face on, giving away nothing to suggest he knew her.

"Gentlemen," Leksik said. "Good to see you all here. Welcome to the Royale." His eyes landed on O'Malley. "You must be Stuart."

"I am. Thanks for the invitation," O'Malley—Stuart—said, his vocal inflection adopting a boyish uptick.

"My associates tell me you have some interest in our business," Leksik said.

"I do. I think I could help you grow your interests in my circle. We're always looking for product we can trust. The Mexican shit is always cut. But I hear you've got grade-A stuff coming in. Something new from Switzerland or some shit."

Leksik pulled his mouth tight and nodded. "Indeed. Perhaps after the game, we can discuss further."

Leksik sat, and Nina sat beside him.

"Who's the piece?" O'Malley said, eyeing Nina suggestively. Nina had to applaud his façade.

He played rich douche well.

"This is Nina. She's a business associate of mine. Nina, you'll remember Olev."

"Yes, hello."

"And his associates, Alexi and Peter. And Stuart Meyers. And this young fellow is Oskar Helk, the son of my very trusted associate out of San Francisco, Anton Helk. He's destined to take over the family business, aren't you? Ambitious kid. Nice to see you, Oskar."

Oskar's dark eyes twinkled, and his sharp features mimicked Leksik's. He cracked his knuckles playfully. "Ready to take your money, Vahtra." His voice was like a California version of a *Goodfellas* extra.

Leksik laughed playfully. "Always the ambitious one. Shall we get on with the game?"

The dealer nodded and dealt out a hand for five-card draw poker.

Nina pulled up her hand, two kings, two eights.

She traded in her lone three and pulled up another eight. Not a bad start.

Oddly enough, Nina had always enjoyed gambling in the high-rollers' rooms. She loved the dry riffle of the cards, and the constant, but modest, drama of the quiet figures around the kitschy green felt. She enjoyed the plush armchairs, the glass of champagne at the elbow, the quiet, unhurried attention of eager attendants. She was amused by both the impartiality of the cards and their eternal bias. From her chair, she was both an actor and a spectator of other people's dramas and decisions, sometimes making life-altering decisions on a 50/50 chance.

Mainly, she liked that everything that transpired was one's own fault. There was only oneself to praise or blame in this room. Luck had to be gracefully accepted or taken advantage of up to the hilt. In this room it was deadly to mistake bad play for bad luck. Luck in all its moods had to be loved and not feared.

Olev ended up with four smiling queens, taking the hand.

Another round was dealt. More drinks were served. Tension tap-danced.

Without preamble, Oskar produced a bag of white powder and a mirror and proceeded to cut delicate lines with a sharp blade. The tap-tap echoed against the crown molding.

He extended it to Nina with a toothy grin. "Care for a little sugar?"

"Thanks, but no. Never touch the stuff myself," Nina said.

She caught Leksik's approving smile out of the corner of her eye.

The game went on. Subtle pressure built up around them with every pass of the cards. It pressed on Nina's lungs until she was afraid she was going to have a panic attack. The ticking bomb was somewhere in this room, and it was only a matter of time before it erupted.

"I'm so glad our organizations have had the opportunity to work together," Leksik said to Oskar.

Oskar grinned widely. "Me too. Dad's thrilled we finally made it all work out."

"It's impressive the way you've taken the reins with such gusto. What are you, eighteen?"

"Nineteen last month," Oskar said.

Leksik smiled with a tinge of wistfulness. "Nineteen. What an age. Your entire life ahead of you. Dreams, desires, all at your fingertips. Not yet scarred by the inevitability of betrayal." Oskar tittered half-heartily, as though the words were the whimsy of a nostalgic old man. "The thing I've been trying to understand, however, is how, with all your resources, you manage to have such incompetent bookkeeping."

Everyone at the table froze, the impending doom lingering. Nina's heart thrummed against her chest cavity. A clock ticked somewhere. Someone swallowed.

Oskar flicked his eyes about, like someone who has not yet realized they are the butt of a joke. "What's that?"

Leksik rubbed his jaw. "Your accounting. Leaves a lot to be desired."

Oskar twisted his face, offended. "Our processes are clean. We never make a mistake."

"Ahh, so then it was deliberate."

Oskar slammed down his cards. "What are you getting at, Vahtra?"

Nina's skin prickled at the boy's insolence.

"Well, I have been trying to figure out what happened to a cool five million your organization was facilitating. Poof, it's just gone. So, either you have terrible accounting, which is unacceptable. Or, you have stolen it. Which is also, as you can imagine, unacceptable."

Oskar's face paled. The truth flashed in his eyes.

"Leksik—I don't know what you're talking about. We would never steal from you."

"Then it's incompetence."

"No, there's no money missing. It's all there."

Leksik put out his cigar and sighed. "I think it's time for everyone to clear the room."

Nina could have heard a pin drop.

"Are you hard of hearing?" Leksik said coolly.

In an instant, everyone had risen except for Oskar.

Nina hopped up from her seat as well.

"Not you, Nina. Your services are needed," Leksik said.

A hard knot formed in Nina's stomach, but she forced a sly smile and sat back down.

The rest shuffled out, leaving only Leksik, Nina, Oskar, and Yegor.

Yegor shut the door and locked it.

Nina saw the raw fear in Oskar's eyes. Where only moments before, he was a cocky young man, now he was reduced to a whimpering child. Terror danced in his dark eyes.

"Please," Oskar started.

But Nina knew they were past the point of negotiations.

Oskar jumped up from his seat, but Yegor was on him in an instant, holding him down.

Nina's heart clenched, but she had to ask herself, didn't he know what he was getting himself into? Wasn't he here by his own design? Wasn't she? No, he was just a kid, raised to be here. His arrogance was a byproduct of his privileged youth, raised by gangsters. He was about to learn a painful lesson.

And Nina was to stand there, smile and nod, offering both her blessing and approval by her complacency.

This was how people morphed into shells of themselves. Small pieces of their soul chipped away, then grew back like a hardened muscle. Until there was no softness left, no humanity, nothing vulnerable or tender to the touch.

Oskar begged. "Please! Please don't kill me!"

Leksik smiled. "Why would I kill you when you owe us money? That's just bad business."

The look in Oskar's eyes turned Nina's stomach. The look of someone who has just realized he will be tortured.

Yegor thrust Oskar back into the chair and deftly tied his wrists to the arms, then his legs. Oskar flailed and screamed, but it was futile against Yegor's massive form.

"Now Oskar, let's be a man, shall we? That is what you've always wanted, isn't it? To be treated like a man?" Leksik said.

"This isn't how you treat a man. It's how you treat animals!" Oskar screamed.

Leksik sighed. "Your generation has such a flair for the dramatic. I think it's YouTube. Everyone thinks they're an actor now."

Yegor retrieved a briefcase and set it on the poker table in front of Oskar. He clicked it open, revealing a rainbow of shining instruments.

"Please, Mr. Vahtra, I don't know what happened to your money. I don't know anything about it." Beads of sweat streamed down Oskar's face.

"Hmm, you see I have worked with your father for two decades. And never once have we had any issues. And then, you come of age and step in, and bam. Five million dollars suddenly vanishes. Poof."

"I can get it back for you, I swear."

"Yes, you will. This is why I won't kill you. Today."

The horrific realization went through Nina's mind that this wasn't an interrogation, this was a punishment. At this moment, there was nothing Oskar could do or say to make it stop.

Oskar closed his eyes in resignation and Nina tried not to do the same. She tried to pretend this didn't bother her.

Yegor pulled a long, serrated knife from the case and examined it, turning it over in the air. Its glint caught in the honey glow of dancing wall sconces.

He turned to Nina and extended it to her with a smile, his hard, steely eyes twinkling with delight—eyes that had glimpsed the Apocalypse and smiled, taking pleasure in the foretold reckoning. A man like Yegor was all but dead inside.

Nina hesitated. She looked to Leksik, who only nodded.

"Why don't you explain to our young friend how things are done in our world?" Leksik said to her.

Nina swallowed a thick lump and accepted the weapon. She glanced to Yegor, not knowing what she was supposed to do.

"What's on the menu?" she said.

Yegor shrugged nonchalantly, as though she'd asked what he wanted to watch on television. "Remove something. I don't care what."

Nina's head throbbed, and her muscles suddenly ached. Bile crept up her throat. Her hands shook.

She couldn't do this.

She examined Oskar, only moments ago a petulant shit. A kid who had practically asked for it. But now he was just a sweating, shaking, child. Would he call for his mother once it began?

She had to do this.

She bit her lip and braced herself. She took a step forward. She leaned closer and met his eyes. She wanted to convey her sorrow, her disgust, at having to do this, but she kept her eyes cold and empty.

She gripped the knife tighter.

"Oskar, why did you steal from us after everything?" Nina said. She gently pressed the point of the blade to Oskar's cheek. She traced under his eye, pressing it into the skin just enough to draw a drop of blood.

Oskar's whole body shook. "I'm sorry. I shouldn't have. I...I needed the money. I had a deal go wrong. And I didn't think you'd miss it. There was so much of it."

*Fucking idiot.* Only someone with a completely false sense of self or a death wish would steal from Leksik Vahtra.

Nina sighed dramatically. "Oh, Oskar, you should have known better. I'm sorry it worked out this way for you, but you asked for it."

"Please," he whispered. Tears streaked his face, his sharp features now somehow soft and boyish in his terror. "Please."

"There are penalties for sticky fingers in this business, Oskar." She grabbed his hand with her own, angling the knife with the other. "It's time to find a happy place."

She bought the knife down to his left index finger.

The scream shattered a piece of her soul.

## 22

Nina's entire body shook. She felt fevered, chilled. She clutched a glass of scotch as she sat on the couch in O'Malley's suite. It likely wasn't the safest place, but she needed to be locked away somewhere out of Leksik's sharp eye.

O'Malley's eyes were sympathetic. "I know, it's rough. Most people would have cracked."

Nina sipped on her drink and shrugged. She couldn't shake the images from her mind. "Whatever. It's part of the job."

"Maybe so. But you don't have to be a robot all the time. You're allowed to feel when no one's looking."

She met his eyes, searched through them, trying to understand him. Who was Shay O'Malley under this façade?

"No, I'm not. You know as well as I do that an undercover needs to lose themselves to win. There is no middle ground."

"Is that how you see all of this? All just a game to win?"

Nina laughed. "A game? No. I see this as a fierce battle

where the stakes are life-and-death. This is a fucking gladiator sport. You know that only one side can win, right? The organization or us. We don't both come out of this alive."

"That's a little dramatic. Operations get pulled all the time. Undercovers stay safe, the bad guys get away. The fight continues another day."

Nina shook her head. "Not in my game. My game is to the death."

"C'mon, Nina. This isn't *Return of the Jedi*. Killing the guy in charge won't immediately end the war."

Nina stood up and refilled her glass from the bottle of scotch on the table. She looked back to O'Malley. "Where'd they find you, O'Malley?"

"You know where. I worked undercover with Graham in L.A."

"You're really young."

"They need babyfaces right out of the academy. They make good undercovers. Like an actor who has a range to his repertoire."

"And why undercover? It's so dangerous."

O'Malley shrugged. "Why not? What have I got to worry about? It's not like I have some pretty little wife and kids. I don't even have parents. Guys like me make the best candidates. Nothing to lose."

"Except your life."

"Maybe life is overrated."

Nina laughed slightly. She half appreciated his cynicism.

"You've known Beck awhile?"

O'Malley smirked. "Yeah. Like six years, I think. Almost know him as well as you."

Nina snapped up. "What the fuck does that mean?"

"Relax, teasing. You'd just have to be blind and dumb

not to notice the attraction between you two. Crackles like a forest fire."

Nina's cheeks burned, and she averted her eyes. She hated her own emotions at that moment. She hated thinking about Beck after what she'd done. He deserved better.

"Relax, Nina. It's not like you can help chemistry. You're both hot. Stakes are high. Not a huge shock you daydream about banging each other. But I know Martinez wouldn't have you guys working together if he thought for a second either of you was stupid enough to do anything about it."

"You think Beck's hot, huh?" she said, diverting.

O'Malley laughed. "I am secure enough in my balls to admit it that yes, he's a fine specimen of a man."

"How old are you, Shay?"

"What does that matter?"

"Just humor me for a moment."

"Thirty. You?"

"Same. But sometimes I feel a hundred. Sometimes I feel like I've lived three lives."

"You kind of have, Nina. I mean shit, you sure know how to pack a lot of action into your average day."

Nina stayed silent for a few minutes. She tried not to think about Oskar's screams of anguish, the smell of blood. The smell of feces as he messed his pants, sobbing. But she didn't think she would ever forget it. Perhaps those few moments had irrevocably changed her.

"What will you put in your report?" O'Malley said.

Nina's skin prickled as she thought about having to relay what happened. Having Beck find out what kind of person she really was.

"The truth. What else can I put?"

O'Malley shrugged. "I don't know, I thought maybe you'd wanna sugarcoat it a little bit."

"For whose benefit?"

"For your own. Wasn't sure you'd want them knowing what you'd done."

"I didn't have a choice, Shay."

He tilted his head. "Didn't you?"

"And what's that supposed to mean?"

"Undercovers have a lot more choices than people like to think. The movies would have you believe that criminals can't wait to put you through some kind of gauntlet of illegal activities to test your merit. Here, shoot up heroin, here fuck this whore, shoot this perfectly innocent person for no good reason. In my experience, just because you're dirty, doesn't mean you're a contract killer. Doesn't mean you're a drug addict. It's a flawed litmus test. Most real criminals wouldn't happily commit first-degree murder just to earn someone's respect."

"So what, I should have said no when Yegor handed me the knife?"

O'Malley shrugged. "Back in the hood, the first response to smelling a cop wasn't to immediately reach for the machete and start hacking. Usually, they clammed up, sputtered and started making excuses. No one was looking to voluntarily kill an agent."

"Yeah, well, that was American ghetto crime. These guys don't follow the same logic," Nina said. "This time, I didn't have a choice."

"Is it what the old Nina would've done?" O'Malley said.

"No, I..." Why had she really done it? Why hadn't she recoiled, run from the room, told Leksik to fuck off and do his own dirty work? Because she had something to prove. Not to Leksik, but to herself.

"What's done is done, okay?" Nina said. "I'll put everything in the report, and Beck and Martinez are just going to have to understand. The guy's alive. He'll be fine. I'm sure you've all done things you're not proud of." She met O'Malley's eyes looking for truth.

O'Malley nodded. "Yeah, we have. Not sure I've ever removed a finger, but hey, first time for everything.

Nina drained her glass and stood. "I think I should go."

"Yeah, okay. Are you ready for this?"

"Ready for what?"

"They're bringing me in on the next deal. Selling me a few pounds. I think we've got our chance. So you've got to be ready for shit to blow up."

"I'm ready. I was ready before I ever got here. Are *you* ready, Agent O'Malley?"

"How's that?"

"Is the case solid? If you go after them on some couple-pound bust, you've blown your hand. They know exactly what ace you have up your sleeve. So, are you ready?"

"Not really up to me, is it? That honor goes to the men behind the curtain. And I think you have their ear more than I do."

## 23

Nina left O'Malley's room and wandered the labyrinth of the casino. The 3 a.m. perfume of smoke and sweat were nauseating. The soul-erosion produced by high gambling— a compost of greed and fear and nervous tension — was unbearable. Her senses woke and revolted from it.

The jingle of slots and the soft crooning of Frank Sinatra in the background did their best to drown out her thoughts, but her inner demons persisted.

She wasn't sure how long she'd meandered, but the gaming rooms were starting to thin out. She rounded a corner and spotted two unlikely characters engrossed in hushed secrets in the far corner of the sport book lounge.

Katja nervously sucked a cigarette, and Aaron Feinstein looked as though he were scolding her about something.

Nina's instincts prickled. Her common sense told her to walk away, but curiosity won out. She doubted there was any legitimate reason those two would be in whispered, clandestine meetings at this hour.

Nina kept close to the wall and slithered into the sport

book in a seat hidden by a Roman pillar. There she watched. Whatever their dealings were, the conversation quickly came to an end, and Katja stormed off. She rushed by Nina, as Nina ducked out of sight. She breathed in and out slowly, trying to steady her rapid heartbeat.

"You know, spying on people is very rude."

Nina snapped up and met Aaron Feinstein's beady eyes.

"So is meeting in secret behind your boss's back," Nina said.

"You don't know the first thing about anything. So mind your fucking business, Cat."

Nina folded her arms and narrowed her eyes. "I can guess what was going on there. Something you don't want Leksik to know about. Striking a secret deal."

Feinstein lunged toward her, sending Nina shrinking back in her chair.

"Listen closely, you're not gonna say a word to anyone about anything. Because you didn't see nothing."

"Something has you a little jumpy, Aaron."

"If you value that pretty skin of yours, you'll drop this."

Nina stood and straightened up. "I don't like being threatened. If you have nothing to hide, then maybe we should let Leksik sort it out."

Aaron smirked. "Fine, go ahead and kick up some dirt, start some drama. It won't get you nowhere. You're just going to seem like a paranoid little girl who has nothing better to do than run around the casino and tattletale on everybody else. Leksik isn't going to appreciate you wasting his time."

Nina pressed her lips into a tight smile. Aaron had a point. She hadn't actually seen anything. But still...she knew a lie when she heard one.

"Fine. Have it your way, Aaron. None of my business,

anyway. But let me give you a little advice. I'd watch your step very carefully. Because if Leksik catches you betraying him, he will skin you alive."

A small flicker of doubt flashed in his dark eyes, but he quickly course-corrected. "I don't need your warnings, little girl. I've been at this a lot longer than you have."

"You're nothing but a pissant, Aaron. A weak, whiny little bitch at the whim of whichever dog is Alpha that day."

Aaron laughed. "What do you know? When I came here in 2000, this hotel was nothing but a crack den, peddling cheap pussy and dollar slots. I built an oasis, an Olympus. A goddamn fucking Valhalla. I had men like Leksik Vahtra begging to work with me. Don't underestimate me for a second."

They stood for a moment at an impasse. Then Aaron straightened his tie and pushed past her.

"Get some rest, Nina. Leksik likes his women perky."

She exhaled a breath she hadn't realized she was holding.

NINA RAN THROUGH WHAT SHE KNEW AS SHE WALKED BACK TO her room. Katja and Aaron were plotting something behind Leksik's back, she was sure of it. Now she had to decide A, whether it mattered and was worth pursuing and B, if it did matter, if telling Leksik was the right move.

Her mind was fractured in a million pieces when she felt the cold presence. She only had a moment to register the sensation before the hand covered her mouth. She screamed futilely into a large leather glove.

She was dragged, quickly and efficiently, around the

corner and into a dark room. Her head smacked into a concrete wall. Her head rang. Metal filled her mouth.

She gathered her thoughts. "What the hell?" She raised her hand to her head, but another smack sent a shock of pain through her skull.

"I warned him you were trouble. I warned everyone," Katja's distinct sharp voice cut through the darkness.

Nina spat blood in her general direction, her eyesight failing both from dizziness and darkness.

A dim light clicked on. They were in a storage room of some kind, dusty crates lining the walls. Katja stood beside a beast of a man Nina recognized as one of Olev's associates. Alexi, Peter, she couldn't remember.

"What the hell do you want?" Nina said.

"What do I want? I want you dead."

"You wouldn't dare kill me. Leksik will kill you."

"No. Leksik will be disappointed to lose his lead into the DEA. But he will move on to other things. Because that is what Leksik does. He doesn't waste time mourning the loss of anything."

"So kill me. Get on with it. But it won't accomplish what you think it will. Leksik already knows you've betrayed him."

"Liar."

Nina shrugged. "Don't take my word for it. Try it out. Doesn't matter to me."

Katja folded her arms over her chest. She was clearly thrown off guard. Had she expected Nina to cower and beg for her life? She didn't doubt Katja was capable of murder, but she didn't think she was stupid enough to carry it out in this situation. Whether or not Leksik actually valued Nina's life, he wouldn't appreciate Katja doing anything behind his back.

Katja took a step forward. She leaned close to Nina. "Consider this your only warning. Stay out of my way. Next time I will kill you."

## 24

L eksik had known betrayal, certainly. But not like this. The fury of it bubbled up inside him like a volcano, molten heat threatening to erupt and destroy everything in its path. He had been foolish to trust her so implicitly. She was always trying to exert her power, consistently overestimating her place in the order or things.

And Leksik would not stand for that. He had tried to guide her, to help her rise in due time, but she was too impatient, too petulant. She had taken advantage of his generosity and patience.

For the life of him, he could not fathom what she'd been thinking. Did she not realize the consequences of such betrayal? Did she believe him so oblivious that he wouldn't find out she was trying to broker deals behind his back? Did she really think that Aaron Feinstein would not stay loyal to the one who feeds him? Foolish girl had so much yet to learn.

There was finally a knock at the door. Leksik nodded for Yegor to open it.

His niece stepped in, looking regal, defiant. She would take her punishments bravely and with pride, he knew this. Katja would not beg or plead. She owned her mistakes, and it was for this he was perhaps willing to forgive much of her trespasses.

For a moment, she stood there dumbly. Finally, Yegor pushed her forward.

She took a few delicate steps and stopped a few feet from his desk.

"Uncle. You wanted to see me?"

Leksik sat up and studied her for a moment before speaking.

"Please sit," Leksik said.

She complied. Her eyes flashed with recognition of the peril to come, but she remained composed.

"Katja, you disappoint me. More than you ever have. I had so much trust in you."

Katja kept her head low, her eyes obedient. Her thin, sharp body shifted.

"Can I ask what I've done to elicit such utter disappointment?"

"Show the integrity to at least admit your betrayal."

"I'm sorry I went behind your back."

"Speak up. And look at me. At least have the decency to look me in the eye while you cower and beg."

Katja raised her sharp blue eyes to meet Leksik's. She lifted her pointed chin. Her serpentine body straightened, her spine slithering into place.

"I am sorry," she said clearly and slowly. "But I will not beg."

"Why did you do it? Do I not provide enough that you seek so much on your own?"

"I was trying to help," she said.

"Help whom? Help yourself? I cannot see what you

hoped to accomplish by this reckless act. You met with dangerous associates and tried to broker a deal. Do you know whose enemy you were negotiating with? You have to understand the delicate treaties we have in place. You compromised everything we have worked for here."

"I thought...I thought it needed to be done. And that you were too distracted to see it."

Leksik went rigid. "You thought I was too distracted to do my job? The job I have done my entire life, while the idea of you had not even been conceived?"

"You have so much on your mind—"

His rage bubbled up. His skin tingled with it. He did not often feel this torrent of emotion, but it came crashing over him in thick, red waves.

"How did you find out?" Katja asked.

"Excuse me? You have the audacity to ask this?"

"I think it's only fair I should know who would betray my confidence. Although I am sure I can guess."

"Don't think you can turn anyone against me. You are a bright young thing, Katja. Brimming with possibility and potential. But you are no match for me. Don't you ever make that mistake again."

"I wasn't trying to betray—"

"Betrayal is only one piece. I have lost faith in your judgment. How can I trust you to do what I ask when you are so reckless? Regardless of your perceived intentions, this was stupid, careless, and selfish. You could have started a fucking war."

Leksik heard his voice as though it were not his own—a lion's roar, fueled by rage and vitriol.

"No one will dare to retaliate," Katja said.

Leksik laughed then. "Oh no? You know nothing then

my child. Frankly, when they do come, I should offer you up as a sacrifice."

Fear flashed in her sharp eyes. She kept her mouth tight.

"But we do not sacrifice our own," he said. Katja's body relaxed. "That doesn't mean there aren't consequences. You wonder why you have not risen as far as you would like? Why you still must do things you feel beneath you? It is because of this stupidity. And there is only one way to manage a misbehaving dog. I should kill you. I should put you down so that I do not have to worry about this again. But you know that I will not this time. Because you are my niece and the blood in your veins means something to me."

Leksik nodded to Yegor. Katja's body stiffened. She would know what would come next.

She took the first punch to the stomach with poise, not making a sound. The next, to her face, had her on the ground. She whimpered slightly but did not cry out. With a kick to her gut, she gurgled blood.

"That's enough," Leksik finally said. "You don't want to kill her."

Yegor stepped back and let Katja regain herself. She coughed blood. She slowly unpretzled herself and pulled herself upright, struggling to stand in her towering stilettos

"Now, I trust that we have a clearer understanding of what you are not to do," Leksik said. Blood pooled around her nose, and her face was rapidly turning purple, but she forced a nod.

"Yes, uncle," she said, her voice hoarse and croaking.

"You will go heal yourself. You will do what I tell you and nothing more. And then when you have thought about your actions, we will discuss a future path for you. Perhaps we can find a place for you to exercise this youthful energy of yours. You may go."

Katja limped toward the door.

"Oh, Katja, go tell Nina I want to see her."

She spun around and glared with fury. "What? Why can't you—"

"Don't. Question. Me. Go fetch Nina."

Ire built to a crescendo in Katja's eyes, but she nodded in obedience and shuffled out.

## 25

Nina rubbed her throbbing head but tried to stay focused on the work in front of her.

"Bingo," she said, elation bubbling up in her chest. This was what they'd been searching for.

She clicked through the threads, reading the beautiful words that might as well have been dipped in gold.

With the help of one of her trusted underground hackers, and a good amount of bitcoin, she managed to access a forum used for communication between Leksik's organization and his suppliers.

She scanned through the various threads, piecing it all together.

*Medical network up and running. 200 doctors statewide on board.*

*Medicaid paperwork in line.*

*Saturn Foods. Statewide produce delivery paid.*

Holy shit, it was a two-pronged approach. Beck had to see this ASAP.

She quickly downloaded the various pages, zipped it into a file, then uploaded it to the encrypted server. She checked the red flag as *urgent.*

Someone pounded on the door. She snapped the computer shut and shoved it under her pillow.

Without waiting for a reply, Katja burst through the door. She was rabid, panting.

Nina jumped up, ready for the defensive. She seethed. "You can't barge in here. What the hell do you want?"

When Nina saw her beaten face, the tears in her dress, she stepped back in horror.

"What did they do to you?" Nina said.

Katja glared hard. "Nothing I did not deserve. And why do you care, kitty cat? Still trying to be the mother hen?"

"What happened?" Nina said again.

"I fucked up, and Leksik is not so happy with me. Why do you care?"

Nina's heart clenched as she took in Katja's beaten face and body. There might be no love lost between them, but they were still women subjected to the whims of powerful men, and for that, Nina felt she owed her a kinship.

"It doesn't have to be like this," Nina said.

Katja cackled. "Are you going to try to save me with your strong superior morality now? Save your beautiful words. I only came in here to tell you Leksik wants to see you. He's in a bad mood so I wouldn't dawdle."

"You don't have to stay and take—"

"You think I'm forced to be here? You think I would CHOOSE any other way? I'm not a weak traitor like you," Katja snapped.

"So you'll keep letting him treat you like this? What if next time they kill you?"

Katja groaned and pushed past Nina and made for the bottle of vodka on the desk. She haphazardly poured some in the glass beside it and slammed it back. She met Nina's eyes.

"Next time I will not be so stupid. That is how it works. You make a mistake, you pay for it. I know the rules and it was my choice to break them. That does not make me a domestic victim, you stupid bitch. It would be the same for anyone."

"Would it? Or does he do it to you because he knows he can?"

"Fuck you," Katja said. She pushed past Nina for the door. Nina grabbed her arm.

"I am just trying to help—"

"You might fool the ones with thick dicks between their legs, but your sweet, compassionate façade doesn't work on me. I've played your game. And I've won. And while you were on the outside getting soft, I've only been sharpening my blade. Leksik will see you for who you are soon enough."

"On the outside? I served time," Nina said.

Katja snickered, then narrowed her serpentine eyes to slits. "My entire life has been a prison sentence, you privileged cunt."

"That kind of language really isn't ladylike," Nina said.

Katja opened the door. "Leksik is waiting."

She slammed the door behind her.

## 26

The smells and sounds of The Black Cat reminded him of her. It was as though he could feel her there, hear her snarky laughter. Smell the floral soap on her skin. These past days without her had felt like an eternity.

"Haven't seen you around in a while," a chipper voice said. Beck looked up to see Nina's blonde Barbie doll-like friend with a coffee pot in hand. She wore the Black Cat uniform well, the small black shorts and tight white shirts molding to her perfectly proportioned curves like a second skin.

He flashed his best smile. "Hey, Brooklyn."

"Aww, you remembered me." Her red mouth beamed.

"Never forget a pretty face. How've you been?"

"Can't complain. If you're looking for Nina, she's out for a couple of weeks. Some kind of family emergency. Right after getting over a bad flu, too. Haven't seen her in forever."

"That's okay, I knew she was out. I actually just missed the coffee," Beck said, smiling. Brooklyn blushed. "Anything besides coffee?"

Beck glanced down at the menu. "How about the protein delight breakfast?"

"Good choice. Up in a flash." Brooklyn turned to go, then stopped. She spun back around. She nervously tucked a lock of blonde hair behind her ear. "Um, I don't think I got the chance to say this, but I wanted to say thanks."

"For what?"

"For basically saving my life." Her cheeks burned red.

Beck lowered his eyes, feeling his own cheeks flush. "Oh. You're welcome. Part of the job. I'm just glad you're all right. You *are* all right, aren't you?"

Brooklyn smiled. "Yeah, every day a little better. I'll grab that breakfast."

Beck watched Brooklyn hop off, hips swaying to the tune of the upbeat music, red Converse tapping along the checkered floor, and had to wonder why a girl like that ever felt the need to stick a needle in her arm. Arguably, they lived in the best time in history. There was an abundance of food, medicine, promise. The chance to see the world, be whatever you wanted.

But then again, sometimes Beck looked around at this world built on social media, insta-celebrity, constant scrutiny where fame is the be-all and end-all because you don't exist unless enough people are paying attention to you, and wondered how the entire world wasn't drugged up to drown it all out. Maybe he was crazy, but was it so much to pine for a world where people occasionally had no choice but to focus on something more crucial than celebrity sound bites and sweatshop fashion?

"Penny for your thoughts, sweet pea," a gruff voice said. Martinez slid into the booth opposite Beck.

"Alert the presses, he does leave the office."

"So this is the scene of the crime?" Martinez said, looking around.

"And what crime is that?"

"The one where Nina removed your balls."

"Fuck you very much as well and good morning to you, sir."

Martinez smirked and picked up the menu. "What's good here?"

"The all meatsie platter might kill you fastest."

"Ahh, just like the son I never wanted."

Brooklyn swished over a moment later with a high-beam smile. She set down a plate of what looked like small beignets.

"Compliments of the house. Nina's recipe. What can I get for you?"

"Coffee and the meatsie platter, please," Martinez said.

Once Brooklyn scampered off, Martinez turned to Beck. "You hanging in there all right? You look wound up. Although that's nothing new."

"You read through the new upload? This is bigger than we thought."

Martinez flubbed his lips beneath his dark mustache. "Yep. It's complex. It's massive fraud. It's all over the place. So first off, they get a whole slew of people to sign up for Medicaid, which basically gives them free medical insurance, free pharmacy benefits, and then they go doctor shopping. Get a bunch of 'scripts from a bunch of different docs and then hit up pharmacies all over town. The docs are in on it—a whole fucking network if this is to be believed—and a couple of well-compensated paper-pushers at Medicaid pushing things through. Then they hit the streets to peddle their wares."

"These guys are ripping off the system. Ripping off the

state taxpayers. Ripping off the goddamn American people," Beck echoed. "Hard to believe they can really get enough supply this way."

"Then second, we've got the stuff coming in through Mexico. Goddamn food supply chain. Shoving heroin into the goddamn asshole of a tomato."

"You buy this story that they're working with the cartels?" Beck asked.

Martinez considered it. "Different product, different market. Maybe they've arranged trade deals on other things to keep the territories in line. Opik is known for arms dealing, human trafficking. We know the cartels also have a radio network that crosses Mexico and the United States in a truly awe-inspiring feat of guerrilla engineering. It's incredibly high-tech, believe it or not. They use constantly evolving encryption, and a repeater network with little stations stuck on top of mountains across the U.S. Rumor has it that the cartels paid a former spec ops comms expert to set it up. Things are a whole lot more fucked if Leksik is tapped into that."

"God, we have to hope he isn't."

"We need to find out who the guy is facilitating the transport from this Saturn Foods Company."

"It's a big company. Responsible for nearly all the cross-state transport," Beck said.

"Better get digging then."

"I think I should go in." The words were out before Beck's mouth could catch up with his brain.

"Sorry?"

Beck leaned in closer. "Maybe I should go in. To The Royale. Act as one of O'Malley's associates. Monitor this thing from the front lines."

Martinez snorted. "Have you had a psyche eval lately?"

"I'm serious."

"So am I. Absolutely not. You'll be made in a heartbeat. You've been hanging around this town too long. Too many people know you."

"The casino is on the other side of the border."

"Doesn't matter. The same players."

"I have a bad feeling. I don't think they should be in there alone without backup."

"Both Nina and Shay are pros. They're fine. They're both making huge strides toward the goal. Be patient and confident in their abilities. We are a phone call away."

Brooklyn returned with their food and a smile. "Anything else for you right now, gentlemen?"

"We're good, thanks Brooklyn," Beck said, flashing a grin. Brooklyn blushed and arched her back just slightly, tipping her ample breasts toward him, a move Beck gathered was instinctual. A girl like that had learned sex was currency a long time ago.

"Ok, just holler if you need anything," Brooklyn said and scampered off.

"To be young again," Martinez said with a nostalgic smirk.

Beck rubbed his jaw, the stubble itching his skin. "All due respect, I think you're wrong on this one. I don't think Nina was ready for this. I think we sent her into a viper pit unprepared."

Martinez refocused on him. "I see your savior complex is alive and well. C'mon, Graham, have you ever lost an asset?"

Her face flashed in his mind. Just a distant memory now, but her wily smile as vivid as if she were right there.

"Yes, we have," Beck said.

Martinez's face crumbled up in contemplation then

relaxed when the memory dawned in his eyes. "Oh, right. The prostitute in Long Beach."

"Don't say it like that. She was a person. A person we failed."

"That wasn't my operation. And the superior on that case was fired."

"Doesn't bring Maria back."

Martinez's bushy black eyebrows went up. "You remember her name?"

"Of course I do. People deserve to be remembered, no matter what their lot in life. And I won't make the same mistake again."

"You will do nothing. The operation is going just fine."

"And if I don't agree?"

"Then hand over your badge. I know you're furious at this thing, Beck. I know it's eating you alive. But this is the job. The job *you* chose. This is why marriages fall apart, why people spend their time curled up to a bottle and not a lover. You knew what you signed up for."

He stabbed a fork into a piece of sausage.

Beck did know what he signed up for. He'd never been able to bear the idea of some mundane paper-pushing job in a soul-sucking gray cubicle. No, he had asked for this, Martinez was right.

But that was when he had nothing to live for. That was when it was just him and his atonement.

What was he living for now?

## 27

K atja was a problem. The hard truth of it sat at the bottom of Nina's gut like a rock. Katja was onto her, and despite how well Nina played it, Katja was cunning enough and smart enough to see right through her facade. Nina's saving grace was that, as of yet, the snake couldn't prove anything.

Katja needed to be dealt with, but how? Nina had to think it through carefully. She couldn't be rash. She couldn't just kill her. Not only would it be her own death warrant, but she also didn't have it in her to take a life in cold blood. Maybe she could find enough evidence against her to out her to Leksik. Then he would take care of the problem for her.

Maybe there was a way to have her arrested. No, that would only compromise the entire operation.

Nina massaged her throbbing temple, trying to quell the incessant thrumming against her skull. What she wouldn't give to just fall into Beck's arms right then. To close her eyes and forget about everything for even just one night.

She groaned and fell back on her hotel bed.

She felt like everything was crashing down. The things she'd done would forever be branded on her. She'd shed blood, she'd taken lives. She'd compromised everything that had ever been good about herself. But didn't the ends justify the means, even a sliver? She had to believe that was true.

Her days here were limited. She was staring down the barrel of a gun, her end inevitable. How much could she accomplish before it all came crashing down?

She wanted to cry frustrated tears. *Just leave me alone!* But she forced herself up and readied to go see the boss.

"YOU KNOW, WHEN I WAS A BOY, ESTONIA WAS IN A SEVERE economic and political crisis. Scarcity of food, medicine, and other basic things. People stood in long lines to buy even essential goods, let alone anything like chocolate. So, who fills this void?" Leksik shrugged and sipped his drink, the clink of the ice echoing in the empty room.

Nina didn't need to answer the rhetorical question. "I know. Luther told me a lot about it. I know it was hard for you all there. Much harder than we here could ever know. But it's gotten so much better the last two decades, right?"

"What is it they call your generation? Millennial?"

Nina blushed and nodded. "Yes, that's what the media likes to label us anyway."

"Labels. So useful, yet so detrimental, don't you think?"

"An age doesn't dictate who you really are. Not everyone is the same at age thirty."

Nina thought of how different her twenties had been from Cammy's. For Cammy, it was college, grad school, a storybook wedding, backyard barbeques and the birth of two cherub babies.

Conversely, Nina had run a drug operation, traveled in the jet-set underworld, then found herself locked behind bars on a federal conviction. Their levels of maturity might vary.

"You often sound like my nephew, did you know that? Your years at his side show."

Nina bit her lip. The question burned, unbearably so. She had to ask. "Is he...is Luther dead, for sure?"

Leksik met her eyes, their dark hooks piercing right through her. "You tell me."

"I...I don't really know for sure. I just know what I'm told. I wasn't there."

Leksik pressed his lips together and nodded. He obviously wasn't going to answer.

"How is Luther your nephew anyway?" Nina asked.

"In your time together, he did not talk about his family?"

Nina shrugged. "He did. A bit. I know he was born in former Czechoslovakia and that his father was from Estonia originally, but I don't know much about it. Was his father your brother?"

Leksik looked as though he were trying to sort out the pieces in his mind. "Luther's father, Petr, was my younger stepbrother. The illegitimate son of my father's third wife, a Czech woman. She was a wretched woman and produced a weak, wretched son. But my father tried to embrace Petr, bring him into the family business. He arranged a good marriage within the family for him. A distant cousin from Czechia, to make my stepmother happy. We had a branch of the family there, you see.

"But he was plagued with weakness. He drank, he hit, he lost control. So, after a time, my father banished him. They fled back to Czechia, and we thought all the better. But when Luther was born, my stepmother insisted Petr bring the boy to visit. My father saw something in him. Something he said was part of us," Leksik tapped his chest proudly.

"So, my father had him come for summers. Then Petr got himself into some gambling troubles he could not escape. He ran to the U.S., taking my nephew. I did not hear from him for many years, and I did not think much about this young boy with frightening eyes. Then one day, I get a call. It's Luther. His papa is in jail, his mama dead, and he wants to come home. We welcomed him into the family."

"And Katja? She said she was Luther's cousin? Your niece?"

Leksik thought again on this, trying to form the connections. His hand drew invisible lines in the air. "Let me think. The snake is my... my father's brother's granddaughter?"

Nina calculated. "Third cousin?"

He laughed and flicked it away. "I don't know. We just call her niece."

Nina's head spun with all the connections.

"Don't worry, I will not test you," Leksik said smiling. "But you should come to understand how we work. It will serve you to respect our dynamics. Blood is everything to Opik. We don't normally bring in outsiders, and this is why my niece is so testy when it comes to you."

Nina snorted. Testy. Right.

"And you never married, had children?" Nina went on.

Darkness crept into Leksik's eyes. His mouth pressed flat.

"I did. Once. She died. More champagne?" Leksik said, holding up the bottle. Nina nodded and extended her glass.

"Do you plan on returning home soon? You must be homesick." Nina wanted to keep him talking, break through his hard exterior.

"Sick is not the word. I am anxious to return home. I

have a lovely estate in Tallinn as you recall. But this is a very beautiful place you have here. I can admit that. And the mountains and trees and the water, the crystal-clear nights and the brisk mornings, they're not so different from home. But what is very different is the people. Soft. Weak. No sense of family or vision."

"A little judgmental, don't you think? It's our grand U.S. of A that makes your business so profitable."

Leksik snorted. "My point exactly. Did you know that Americans consume eighty percent of the drugs produced in this world? Eighty. You are gluttonous, fat, over-privileged, and self-righteous and I have no qualms about taking you down."

"Well, at least you're honest," Nina said, hiding her laugh with her champagne flute.

"You live in a world that idealizes skank celebrities who let their bits hang out on social media. You don't admire people who fight, you admire people who Tweet. And because you have no reason to work for anything, you don't. You toss your elders out on the street. You don't care for your people who are ill. What kind of country is this, anyway?"

Nina's defense of her homeland came to attention. But she couldn't argue some of his points. She did worry that the country had lost itself. She worried that the abundance of everything had become their own worst enemy. She'd read that humans were psychologically and biologically wired to consume. Like animals, wired to eat what's in front of them, consume what gives them instant gratification. Unfortunately, their biology hadn't caught up with their societal abundance.

But it was a country where people could be free. Where people like Beck fought tooth and nail against corruption and human plagues like Leksik Vahtra.

But she just shrugged playfully.

"I suppose we're a little spoiled," Nina said.

"And the thing is, we come in, we make money off you, and you don't care. Because you want your drugs, and you want them cheap. Do you know how cheap heroin is now on the streets? Pretty little white pills? Ten times the prices, but fancy housewives and rich college kids will still pay it because it makes them feel better about themselves. But it's all the same thing. No matter who is buying, we have a product for them. If you are homeless begging for change, whoring yourself out for your next fix, you can still afford it. If you are a rich housewife in one of these big mansions on the lake looking for something to dull your vapid existence? We have a pill for that. You are a country ripe with customers just waiting to self-destruct."

*We're also a country ripe with law enforcement spending every moment and resource on taking you down*, Nina thought. But she didn't voice her opinion.

"What have you told the Feds so far?" Leksik said.

Nina snapped to attention, caught off guard. Leksik had a way of lulling away your guard, then throwing questions at you while you were unprotected.

Nina swallowed hard. "I gave them the information you said to. About the drop."

Leksik nodded. "Good, good."

"I still don't understand. If they show up to an empty deal, they'll know you're feeding me false intel."

"Who says it will be empty?"

"Are you planning on killing them? Is this a trap?" Her pulse quickened.

Leksik cocked an eyebrow. "And would you care?"

"Yes, I would. I am in this for the money. I don't believe in senseless murder."

Leksik smiled lightly. "Such sentiments. But don't worry. I don't either. Killing Feds is something I actually try to avoid. The cartels tried it once, and Uncle Sam rained down the apocalypse. But the drop is not empty. It is merely a, what did you call it? A red herring. They will find a treat when they arrive."

"You're sacrificing someone."

Leksik shrugged. "Only someone who deserves it."

"But won't it lead them right to you?"

"Don't worry so much about the details, Nina. It's all taken care of. The Feds will have a crumb to keep them down the path we want. And while their resources are distracted elsewhere, we do our final deal."

"And me?"

"You'll come with me, of course. You have proven yourself very effective. Olev was impressed by you. Greatly. And he doesn't take to women often."

Shocking, Nina thought, picturing the lecherous prick.

"Who are you sacrificing?" Nina said.

"Not your concern. Just someone who has earned their place as the lamb."

Leksik stood and walked to the bar in the corner. "Now, enough of this. Let us celebrate our victories. Let us plan for the future and dream." He pulled a new bottle of Louis Roederer Cristal Champagne from the cooler and deftly popped the cork.

He came back to her and filled her glass with liquid the color of rose gold. "I see a great future ahead for us."

"Us?"

"I think, Nina, we could have a fruitful relationship. A bond."

Nina's heart quickened its pace. He rested his hand on her shoulder. A chill crawled up her spine. She pressed the champagne flute to her mouth. She tried to focus on the smoky taste of the French bubbles and not the pounding of her heart.

"Fruitful," she echoed. "That may be, but I think I'm still bound for a remote island somewhere when this is over."

She tried to sound light-hearted, careless. Leksik squeezed her shoulder.

He leaned closer to her. His hot breath tickled her neck as his lips brushed the pulsing skin. "Don't run away just yet. There could be so much more between us, Cat."

His hand moved from her shoulder, down her arm and around her belly.

Nina forced herself to face him. She wasn't going to play coy. Wolves like Leksik responded to a firm stance.

"I thought you were involved with Katja. Your...niece."

Leksik stiffened, then snickered. "Katja is a child. A dreamer. Impulsive. She has kept me company, but I think our time together draws near."

Nina's stomach turned over. She couldn't imagine allowing him to touch her. She stood and lifted her chin.

"I think I should go. It's getting late."

Leksik smirked. He took her hand. He stroked the skin delicately with his finger. "Come, now. Let us not play games. I can give you much."

Nina jerked her hand away. "Your nephew. He loved me. Doesn't that mean anything to you?"

Leksik shrugged. "Where is he now?"

"I don't know, Leksik. Why don't you tell me?"

Leksik narrowed his dark eyes at her. She wanted to squirm under his gaze, to run. She stayed still. She stared him down.

"You love him still?" he said.

"I..." What did she say to that? "I don't know how I feel

anymore. I don't think it matters. Our time together has passed. But I would still honor his memory. And I'd think you'd do the same."

Leksik smiled thinly. "You're a loyal woman, Nina. I commend you." He sighed and went back to his desk. "Go. We have a long day tomorrow."

Nina waited for an addendum, but Leksik turned his attention back to his computer, not sparing her another look.

## 28

**B**eck had high regards for his own life, but the fear of death wasn't the hardest part of law enforcement. He could end up getting someone's lover killed. Someone's child. Someone's friend. Someone he loved. He found out fairly quickly that another person dying on his watch was far worse than the specter of his own death.

Beck knew he might be out of his mind, but he didn't care. He had a bad feeling about this whole operation. Something wasn't right, and that feeling sat in his gut in a hard lump.

The bust was supposed to be easy. All laid out for them.

And it was.

That was the problem. Busts were never that easy.

Anton Helk—long-time San Francisco gangster was in Tahoe to complete a deal with a Nevada branch of the Sonora Cartel, possibly on behalf of Leksik Vahtra. According to Nina's intel, they were meeting in a secure warehouse location at a small private airport on the California side to transfer some multiple tons of narcotics.

And they'd been there, unloading crates of soup cans from a Mexican relief aid propeller plane, not a care in the world. Sitting ducks.

Beck's team had seized 850 pounds of meth, nearly a ton of cocaine, 93 pounds of heroin, and almost 50 pounds of pharma-grade opioids. $1.42 million in cash topped off the kitty. They'd arrested 22 people, both Sonora and from Helk's crew.

The rage on Helk's face when the DEA descended told Beck he'd been betrayed. He went quietly, without a fight, vengeance stirring in his dark eyes.

The takedown had been far too easy. A high-ranking gangster like Anton Helk wasn't that negligent. He'd run clean operations out of San Francisco for a decade, then just gets picked up carelessly? No, Helk had been sold out. Leksik had sacrificed him.

And that meant while Beck's team was picking off low hanging fruit, Leksik had something bigger unfolding behind the curtain. Nina had to know about it. She was too smart not to see right through it.

And that posed a question: Was Nina playing him? He couldn't believe that she was capable of that level of betrayal. But his nagging doubt wouldn't relent.

Martinez would kill him for being there, but Martinez didn't have to know. Beck had been in more dangerous situations than this; he could handle himself. Just get in, get some info, get out. Even if he was made, they weren't going to needlessly kill a DEA agent.

He hoped.

He caught a glimpse of himself in the mirrored door as he entered The Royale Luxury Casino and Resort. He'd slipped on his favorite charcoal suit—the one he felt gave him just a dash of luck. At least, he looked as though he belonged there.

The casino buzzed with glittering lights and ringing laughter. Even in the early hours, people had lost themselves in debauchery, the disillusioned idea that they might be here to make their fortune. Just like so many fortune hunters before.

Beck tried to focus on the people he passed all at once but also not make eye contact or be noticed. He needed to blend in. Just a business guy here for a conference, to play a few hands, unwind. He mindlessly stroked the counterfeit Sacramento Area Medical Association badge around his neck.

His eyes darted back and forth, continually scanning. His ears perked up, trying to sort through the sounds, isolating anything that could be of importance.

He had no idea if he would even be able to find her. In the sober light of day, he was starting to realize this was a half-cocked plan at best. Even if Nina was in the Casino at this moment, she was probably locked away in her rooms, not aimlessly roaming the pit. And even if she were, she'd never be out of Leksik's line of sight.

Perhaps this was a failed mission before it even began.

He passed by a myriad of well-heeled men and cheap women, too much glitter, too much gloss. It was a stark contrast to the laid-back, serene oasis that was Tahoe Village, just two miles down a mountain road.

And then, out of the corner of his eye, Beck saw something unexpected. He casually strolled up to the young man in the sport coat, leaning against a Roman pillar.

"Stuart," Beck said, casually, confidently.

Stuart—O'Malley—snapped around. His eyes went wide.

"Dude. What are you doing here? What's wrong?" O'Malley said in a low voice.

"Just checking in. What's the deal? What went down yesterday?"

"What are you talking about?"

"We were sent on a false mission. A red herring. You know it as well as I do," Beck said.

"What? I don't know what you're talking about."

"You know nothing about the Helk arrest?"

"What that kid, Oskar? What he get popped for?"

"Not the son. King Daddy. Anton Helk."

O'Malley's expression was tight. Beck searched his eyes for truth. They'd been in the trenches together. Side by side, each other's lives in one another's hands.

O'Malley leaned in. "Look, I heard maybe Leksik was setting up some guys to take the fall. Some guys that crossed him. Stole some money. Didn't you get Nina's report?"

"About the deal?"

"About the Oskar kid."

Beck's blood went cold. "No, what happened?"

O'Malley chewed his lip. "Shit got rough. Nina...she cut off the kid's finger."

Beck's balance faltered. He leaned against the pillar. "What? Why?"

O'Malley shook his head. "She had to. It was...look you should talk to Nina about it."

"Love to. Where can I find her?"

"You shouldn't be here, Graham. You're gonna blow the whole thing. Get us all killed."

"There's back up," he lied. "Everyone's safe."

O'Malley snickered. "I've been knee-deep in your bull-shit long enough to recognize the smell, Graham. Look,

Nina's on the Penthouse floor. Got a suite near Vahtra's. She's well-guarded. You won't get to her unnoticed."

"But you can."

O'Malley paled. "What? No way. I can't. They don't know I know her outside of casual business. I'd have no reason."

"Then you'll have to get her out of her rooms. Get a message to her. I'll book a room. You tell her where to go."

"How am I supposed to do that?"

"C'mon, Shay. You've been here for months. You've been working with Nina for weeks. You got this."

Beck patted O'Malley on the back. "I'll text you my room number. You can do it, kid."

Beck paced the hotel room. Any number of things could be keeping her, he knew that. Maybe O'Malley was right, and he couldn't actually get a message to her. Maybe Nina couldn't leave her room. Maybe she didn't want to. He walked to the window and stared out at the stormy landscape. The panorama of evergreens and gray skies stretched as far as the eye could see. It was breathtaking. He looked around his hotel room. Its opulence was unrivaled, but it stank of blood and rot.

A gentle knock at the door startled him. His heart raced. He breathed in and out a few times. Probably just housekeeping. Or O'Malley there to offer his condolences.

Or Leksik there to put a bullet in his head.

He shook off his anxiety and gingerly opened the door. His heart nearly stopped.

Nina shrieked, then slammed her hand over her mouth. Her green eyes went wide.

"Beck! What the hell are you doing here?" She snapped in a whisper.

He grinned. He couldn't help it. The sight of her nearly knocked him off balance.

"I had to see you. I was dying."

"You might just die if they catch you. You're an idiot."

He pulled her into the room and shut the door. For a moment they stood there, caught in each other's gaze, breath heavy. "I know, I know. But I have a bad feeling about the way this thing is going. O'Malley told me what happened. Are you all right?"

"Dammit, Shay. He said he wouldn't."

"You really thought about keeping that from me? Jesus, Nina. That's fucking traumatic. And not to mention, I don't know..."

"You going to arrest me?"

"What? Of course not. I don't know what's going to happen, but you did what you had to do to keep your cover. Are you all right?"

"I'm fine. You shouldn't be here."

"You said. But I couldn't stop myself."

"Stop grinning. This isn't a joke." She folded her arms over her chest.

She was different somehow. A little harder. Her green eyes were sharper, glinting. She looked thinner, her toned arms all sinew protruding from her tight black dress. Her dark hair was pulled back in a high ponytail, its ends curled. Her thin legs ended in sharp heels. It was hard to reconcile the rebel girl in motorcycle boots and ripped jeans with this femme fatale.

"I don't think anything about this is funny, Nina."

"Beck, you need to leave."

"No, Nina. What I need is you."

He pulled her close, needing to feel the heat of her body, needing to know she was still her. He pressed his mouth to hers, savoring her.

She relented for a moment but then quickly pulled away.

"Beck, you can't. We can't."

Something was off. She was edgy, tense. "Nina, what is it?"

"It's nothing. I just can't do this. I need to focus. I can't afford to get emotional right now."

"Stop."

"Excuse me?"

"Stop putting on this bullshit persona. For just a moment, be yourself."

She blinked. Her green eyes shone with a thin veil of glistening tears. "I can't."

Beck stepped closer and slid his arms around her waist. He pulled her close. "Yes, you can. Do it for me."

He pressed his mouth down on hers again. This time she didn't pull away. Like the first time he'd ever kissed her, a shock ran up his entire body. She fell into him. She tore at him. Hunger roared inside him as he devoured her.

She pushed his jacket down his arms as he assaulted her neck with his mouth. The heat from her body penetrated his skin. He picked her up—she was just a feather in his arms—and carried her to the bed. He threw her down and fell on top of her. He tore the tight dress from her body, his skin burning at the sight of her long, lean muscles and firm, round breasts. He ran his mouth up her skin. She bucked and moaned, her fingers digging into his back. The need for her pulsed through him, invading every conscious thought. She opened her legs for him, eager. He pressed a finger inside her, then another. She tightened around him. Then she flipped them both over, straddling him. Feral, raw hunger stirred deep in her eyes. She lowered herself onto him, and he nearly cried out.

The pleasure built up like a bullet in a chamber desperate to fire. Her hands scored his chest as the speed of his thrusts increased. He clutched her and pulled her down tighter, harder. He felt the pounding in the pit of his stomach, felt her inner muscles tensing around him. She made him feel like an animal, primal.

Her moans increased, and with a shudder of her body, it brought him to the edge. She cried out, bucking and arching back. Her dark hair fell from its confines, tumbling around her shoulders. Panting and sweating, she collapsed onto his chest and closed her eyes.

NINA WOKE TO THE SOUND OF GENTLE BREATHING, CALMING like a lake breeze. She let one sleepy eye flutter open, then the other. The foggy morning peeked in at their naked forms through the small slits in the diaphanous blinds. He lay beside her, all lean muscle and sinew kissed with scars; a sliver of imperfection. Her hand found its way to the arm encasing her, and she let her red nails skim the ink swirling around its massive bicep.

She was angry at herself for falling asleep, but the muse of dreams had taken her before she could argue.

She laid there simply breathing Beck in. The scent of leather and sweat assaulted her senses—the scent that was uniquely his. Their time together was increasingly precious, each sliver of a moment stretching out, transcending normal time until they were lost in a distant plane. She grasped tightly to the soft cadence of breath and the heat of his skin against hers because she knew their time dwindled with each passing breath.

It was never enough. Every moment was a lifetime and also a blink. She feared this was how they were destined to live out their days; forever grasping as one of them slipped away at dawn to do what they must in the world. Nina would never fully hold him, fully possess him. Or him, her. They were both the kind of people others would always try to catch. But it was still worth it. Even one moment with him was worth a lifetime with anyone else.

Beck's eyes peeled open, and his lips turned up when they focused on her.

"I think I might love you," he said. The words came out crisp and deliberate.

Nina blinked, her chest tightening. Love. He loved her. How could that be? She didn't know how to receive love any more than she knew how to give it. She had never really loved.

With Luther, it had been different. It had been an obsession, an addiction. But not love.

Did she love Beck? Undeniably. And that was their curse.

She rolled over and hid her face. She couldn't let him see her cry.

Nina pulled herself from bed and fumbled for her things.

"Promise me you won't come here again," Nina said. "You can't be here. I don't care what you think you're going to accomplish. If you have to send someone in, you send someone else." She slipped on her lacy black panties and matching bra.

"Nina—"

"I mean it, Beck. I've never been so serious about anything in my life."

His hand traced the skin of her back and fingered the delicate French lace of her under things.

"I just noticed these," he said.

She turned to face him. "What?"

"The sexy lingerie. Where'd you get it?"

She blinked a few times. "What are you talking about?"

Beck pushed himself up. The blankets fell from his naked torso, his tanned skin glowing with the sheen of sweat.

"You didn't know you were coming to see me. So why were you wearing lacy black underthings? Did Leksik give those to you?"

Nina laughed incredulously. "I can't believe this."

"It's a fair question, considering."

"Considering? No, it's not." She thrust up from the bed and found her dress on the floor. "Not that I should have to defend myself, but I'm not sleeping with Leksik, if that's what you're implying."

He reached for her, but she yanked away. "Nina, I—"

"Just don't, Beck. Ok? Just…just leave right now and don't come back. Wait an hour, then get out of the casino. Don't contact me again. It's not safe."

She slipped into her heels and headed to the door.

She was certain she heard his heart breaking apart in rhythm with hers.

## 29

Carefully, Nina left Beck's room, checking every nook and cranny as she slipped down the hall to the elevator. She made it back to her room practically panting from anxiety. She shut the door and leaned back against it as though she was nailed there. She breathed in and out a few times. Everything was all right. She was safe. Beck would be safe.

She quickly retrieved her computer from the secret compartment and pulled up the encrypted browser. Her fingers stroked the keys, wanting so desperately to type the words that were in her mind. *Martinez, you have to keep Beck away. It's not safe.*

But could she really do that to the man she loved? It could cost him his job. But what was more important, Beck keeping his job or his life?

"Goddammit!" She screamed into her fist. He was too damn reckless. "Goddammit."

Her whole body shook; she felt tears pricking at the back of her eyes. What the hell was she going to do? How was she ever going to get out of this alive?

She picked up the burner phone O'Malley had put in her pack with strict instructions not to use except in case of emergencies. In her opinion, this was life and death.

She quickly typed out a message to Beck's number.

*Please text me when you're safe.*

She quickly deleted the text history and threw the phone onto the bed and sighed.

A knock at the door startled her. What she wouldn't give for just a few uninterrupted hours to think.

She shoved the laptop back into its hiding place and ran to the door. She opened it just a crack. Yegor filled the entry.

"What's up?" She said, her voice coming out groggy and cracked. She was too exhausted to play her role properly.

"Get dressed. It's time."

"Time for what?"

"A meeting. With Leksik."

"Thought I had the day off."

Yegor rolled his eyes at her flippancy. "Change of plans. Be ready in twenty minutes. Come to Leksik's room."

Nina was in a daze, but she forced herself to find composure. She jumped in the shower for a quick two minutes to wash the scent of Beck off of her, as much as she hated to do it. She wanted to bathe in that scent forever. Then she threw on one of her standard black dresses and heels. She applied a quick layer of makeup and ran some mousse through her messy hair to tame her bed head into an intentionally tousled look.

"Good enough," she muttered into the mirror, trying not to look at the woman who stared back at her.

She scuttled down the hall toward Leksik's suite. Her nerves were frayed. Her composure was cracking. She didn't know how much longer she could do this.

Yegor let her into Leksik's room and shut the door firmly.

Something was unsettled in the air. A hard, thick knot formed in her gut. The room was empty, except for Leksik and Yegor.

Leksik sat at his desk, his face a cold, stone mask.

A pinch started at the base of her spine and deliberately crawled its way up each vertebra. Her knees threatened to buckle. She was unsteady, her legs Jell-O.

"You wanted to see me. Something about a meeting," Nina said. Her voice trembled, betraying her.

Leksik stood from his desk and walked to her. He cracked his neck and loosened his tie. Nina instinctively stepped back.

"I'm not sure I know what to say," Leksik said.

Nina swallowed. A million thoughts raced through her mind. Oh, God. This was it. She was going to die.

She took another step back but bumped into Yegor's massive frame. His enormous hands fell on her shoulders, holding her tightly in place.

Leksik made his way to her, stopping inches from her. He gently stroked her hair, then his grip tightened, fisting his fingers through her tangled waves. She winced as he yanked her head back.

"I should kill you right now."

"For what?" She said defiantly.

At that, Leksik laughed. "For what, she says. Did you hear that, Yegor? She's going to play dumb."

Leksik turned his head back to her. She felt the impact of his hand on her cheek. The sting came a moment later. She winced, but she would not cry out.

"Don't cry, Nina. That's just a little tap to remind you that you're still alive. For now."

"What do you want?" Her head was ringing.

Leksik stroked her hair again, curling a lock around his finger. "That's a good question. What do I want?"

He backed away from her and looked up at the ceiling, rubbing his head. "What I want is to be able to fucking trust people. But apparently, that is far too much to ask of this world."

He snapped back around and glared at her. "What is it with you women? You demand to be taken seriously, to be given equal rights, but then you go and betray us the moment our guard is down."

"Maybe that should tell you something about women, Leksik. Don't let your guard down."

Leksik chuckled. "Oh, don't I know it? First Katja, then you. I almost expected it from Katja. She's young and impulsive enough to think she could get away with going behind my back. But you, Nina. You I thought better of. I had respect for your intelligence. I was wrong. And I hate to be wrong."

"I don't know what you're talking about," Nina said.

"Really? You aren't undercover, planted by the DEA?"

Nina said nothing.

He walked back over to her. His hand shot up to her neck, long fingers, wrapping around her throat. He squeezed, applying slow, steady pressure. His grip tightened, choking the breath from her.

She struggled, but Yegor held her tightly. Her vision started to blur and blacken. It wouldn't take long, she knew. Just as the sharp pain seared the back of her eyes, Leksik eased his grip.

He smiled. "What do they know?"

Nina coughed. "I don't know what you're talking about."

His hand went back to her throat, and he started again.

"What do they know?" he repeated slowly. "Nina, I don't want to do this. I've never enjoyed hurting women."

"Then don't," she barely choked out.

Leksik laughed again. "I will never tire of your courage, my dear. I'll ask you again. What do they know?"

"I haven't told them anything." Her words were strained, whispered.

"And why is that?"

Nina could barely think as the breath escaped her. "Because I haven't had anything to tell them."

"But you were planning on it, weren't you? To leak whatever you could to the DEA?"

"Does it matter what I say at this point?" She choked out. "You're going to kill me one way or another."

Leksik released his grip. She sucked in a breath.

"Not yet. The young agent. You fucking him?"

Nina's heart raced. Beck. How did they know about Beck? She bit down on her tongue. She wouldn't give in.

Yegor grabbed her arm and twisted it back. White hot flames seared her muscles. She cried out, unable to stop her reflex. She wanted to collapse, but Yegor held her up. Tears pierced her eyes. Her whimpers morphed into growls.

She breathed through it. "Get off on hurting little girls, Yegor?" she croaked out.

"Not so little," Yegor said.

Leksik gave Yegor a curt nod, and he relented his grip on her. Her arm dropped, and she clutched it to her chest. She gave it a wiggle. It wasn't broken, but it was going to hurt.

"Take a seat, Nina. Catch your breath. There is something I want to show you."

Nina pulled herself up and flopped into a chair.

"Good. Stay there. I will be right back."

With that, Leksik and Yegor both left.

## 30

I t was an eternity before Leksik returned. She paced his suite, wanting desperately to spy and pry but knowing every square inch of the room would be monitored. Her arm ached, her jaw throbbed, her mind was fractured into a million pieces. She had to keep it together.

Finally, she heard the door and froze.

It was Yegor.

"Where's Leksik?" she said.

Silence.

"Yegor! What's going on?"

"Come with me."

"No. I'm through with your intimidation games. I'm not going anywhere with you. Where the hell is Leksik?"

"You are a huge pain in my asshole." He grabbed her injured arm and yanked. She shrieked.

"Okay, I'm sorry, I'm coming."

He released her, and she followed him out of the suite obediently.

They walked down the hall then to a side door that

looked like a maintenance room. An elevator took them down, descending each floor with painful precision.

"Where are we going?"

"Shut up."

Finally, the elevator dinged, and they stepped into a staff corridor. She smelled bleach and cleaning products. She heard the low hum of commercial machinery and Spanish chatter.

Yegor pushed her along, finally leading her to another room. He opened the door and shoved her in.

"What are you doing?" Nina seethed. The room was a shade lighter than pitch dark. She blinked, trying to adjust. Yegor shoved her down and her ass collided with wood.

"Just sit down and shut up for once. We have something to show you."

Yegor thrust open a curtain revealing a two-way mirror into another room.

In the other room was Beck.

Tied to a chair.

Leksik stood over him.

## 31

There had only been a few times in Beck's life when he'd been terrified of something. He had been through enough, he'd suffered enough physical pain, to not fear the actual pain itself. It would hurt, yes. It would be possibly more than he thought he could stand. But he knew he was strong enough to survive it if his mind could stay strong. They say it's not the physical pain that lasts in torture victims. It's the psychological trauma. The body forgets pain; it remembers the threat of pain, the reasons behind the pain.

Beck once delivered a baby in Afghanistan in a bombed-out back alley bunker. The mother nearly died. She screamed blood-curdling shrieks as the baby ripped through her body, barreling into the world. But once she held the child in her arms, it was as though the pain had never happened. It had all been worth it because she now held a beautiful piece of herself. Her painful sacrifice was to create life.

But it was different with torture. That pain is inflicted for purely sadistic and psychologically damaging reasons. And so that pain lingers forever in your subconscious.

He had witnessed such things on both sides of the fight. He'd seen it in combat. He'd seen it in undercover. He'd been forced to be a bystander in both worlds.

But now, he sat on the receiving end. The overhead neon lights flickered in rapid, disjointed staccato. He smelled bleach and piss.

Leksik Vahtra examined Beck's wallet. "Frank Watson of Sacramento," he said in a fake American accent.

He met Beck's eyes and snickered. "Here for the convention? That's a weak cover, my friend. Boring. But we both know who you really are. Special Agent Graham, DEA. Oh, don't bother trying to deny it. We have some pretty advanced software. Facial recognition." Leksik pulled a piece of paper from his jacket pocket and showed it to Beck.

A print out of his DEA badge. Fuck.

"So?" Beck said.

"DEA. So fond of yourselves, aren't you? So arrogant. You might think that you live in the land of prosperity and freedom. But there is more violence in this country than in war-torn third-world nations."

"You people are animals."

"You kill each other for breakfast, and you think we're the animals? Guns, drugs, prostitutes—It's easier to get these things here than anywhere in the world."

"Maybe you should go home then. Back to all your safety and morals."

Leksik smiled thinly. "Trust me, friend, I cannot wait. It's a shame you and I are on opposite sides. Men like you—loyal, brave, capable—are not so easy to find."

"Just call us star-crossed," Beck said.

"Maintaining your sense of humor. I appreciate that. You're going to need it."

Leksik paced the room, rubbing his sharp jaw.

"I will make this simple, Agent Graham. Just tell me what I want to know. What are you doing here?"

"Just wanted to check out the world-class resort. Maybe make a few bucks at the table."

"Now is really not the time for that adorable charm of yours." Leksik leaned in close. "Now is the time for honesty. What are you doing here?"

"Scoping the scene. Aaron Feinstein is on our radar for tax fraud."

"But you're DEA, not FBI."

"You know the difference? Smart boy."

"And Nina? She's your accomplice?"

Every nerve and muscle in Beck's body came to attention. He willed his expression to stay calm. He laughed lightly. "Sullivan? Hardly. She's more likely to work with you guys than us."

Leksik nodded, amused. "So, you haven't seen her? She's not working with the DEA?"

"No. We tried, but she wasn't having any part of it. So, we let it go. I think she's mad at us for killing her boyfriend. Hey, were you related to him? I'm really sorry about that."

Leksik smirked. "Such wit. I suppose next you will deny fucking her."

"Only in my dreams, Vahtra."

Leksik smirked "Hmm. You will sing the truth soon enough, agent."

Beck's heart raced. Where was Nina now? Did he have her locked up somewhere?

The door to the room opened, and a massive man stepped in.

"Ah, Yegor. Thank you for joining us. I think it's time to get the party started."

Beck eyed Yegor as he walked in slowly, like a yeti. People conducted interrogations and inflicted torture for many reasons. To save lives, to get secrets, to stop wars. Beck stared into the dark empty eyes of his would-be punisher. He saw the ire, the malice, the empty pits. This man did not have the greater good at stake. He did not have a higher power or sense of morality. This man was doing what he was doing because he took pleasure in the act. Because they paid him well. Because a man with no soul has limited job opportunities.

Yegor set a bag on the table and pulled out his collection of tools. Beck recognize some of them. Staples of the trade. Some looked rather creative.

He tried to breathe steadily. He tried not to think about it. Tried to brace himself against what he knew was coming. Because they would ask him things that he could not speak of. They would want answers he could not give. They would want him to betray those he could not betray. He would rather be torn piece by piece, flayed alive, than betray Nina or Martinez.

Yegor smiled at him, his teeth off colored and crooked.

"Now, we are going to have some fun," he said, his accent unmistakably Russian.

"I bet we are," Beck said, keeping his tone light, his smile easy.

"You are going to tell me everything I want to know. Because I can outlast you."

"We'll see. I have incredible endurance."

Yegor sniggered. "Cocky. I like that. Makes it all the more fun to break you. I hate to waste my time on the weak." He gently laid out his tools with loving delicacy.

Leksik ran his hand along the instruments. "From concentration camps to war, history proves that people can survive unspeakable traumas. Yet there is no neat and tidy explanation as to how they do it. You just don't die. You have no idea what atrocities the human body can endure. It is the most resilient of God's creations. Pain, starvation, cold. Yegor here once spent three days in a pit of snow in a Russian prison, naked."

Beck met Yegor's dark eyes. "Congratulations."

Yegor smiled thinly. "You will beg me for your life. You will beg me and promise to do anything for me to stop. You will beg to suck my cock."

"Only if you promise to enjoy it."

Yegor slugged him in the jaw. Beck grunted as his head slammed back. He regained his composure and met the man's eyes.

"Well let's get on with it then," Beck said.

"If you'll excuse me, gentleman, I think I'll observe from the front row, with Nina. Enjoy," Leksik said. "Oh, and Agent Graham. I'd start talking before you're ready. Because he won't stop until long after you've capitulated."

Beck closed his eyes and breathed in and out a few times. He would go to another place. A place with Nina. He would survive because Nina and the operation were counting on him. He would survive because he and Nina had a future to see.

Yegor pulled out a knife, its blade catching in the neon overhead lights. He pointed it at Beck's eye and grinned. Then he set it back down. Beck exhaled.

"Let's not damage your pretty face just yet. That might piss you off a little too much."

Beck snorted. "Yeah, thanks for the consideration."

Yegor pulled out what looked like a modified taser. He

ripped open Beck's dress shirt and looked hungrily at his exposed torso. Beck steadied himself, breathed.

The smell of fire and rot filled the room as the electric wires made contact with his flesh.

A feral growl escaped his mouth, but he kept his jaw tight.

Yegor pulled away. "Is Nina your informant?"

Beck met Yegor's eyes. "Nope."

"Hmm. We'll see."

Yegor pressed the wires to his flesh again. Beck screamed.

## 32

Nina wanted desperately to close her eyes against the horror unfolding in front of her, but she couldn't. She needed to bear witness to the pain she had caused. It was her fault he was here. She should have never allowed him to get close. Katja was right. Love was a weakness. Nina was death.

Leksik stroked her hair. She didn't squirm. She wouldn't give him the satisfaction.

Beck's screams tore through her mind, burning.

"A sweet song," Leksik said. "Are you happy with yourself, Cat?"

She clenched her jaw to contain her venom.

Leksik started to pull her up, but she resisted. "Come. It's time to go."

"No. No, I need to be here," Nina yelled.

"Trust me, you don't want to watch the rest."

Nina felt like she was going to pass out, vomit, rage, die. But she couldn't leave.

"You're a bastard."

"Literally? No. But I get your meaning." He yanked Nina

up. "Come. You and I have business. You're going to tell me exactly what the DEA knows. And if you don't, Yegor will start removing skin. Graham's. Not yours."

He pulled her from the room. She caught one last look at Beck. His gaze turned toward the glass, and for a moment, she swore he smiled at her.

It will be all right. They would both survive.

Leksik dragged her back up to his suite, staying silent despite the vitriol she spat. She was losing herself, losing all self-control. Nothing mattered.

He thrust her into a chair and zip-tied her wrists to the arms. She didn't struggle. She didn't want him to use tighter bonds.

Leksik stood. Anger, frustration, exhaustion warred on his features. Could she possibly frustrate him to death?

"Now what?" Nina asked.

"Now you're going to sit there for a few minutes while I have a drink. Dealing with you is exhausting." Leksik poured himself a vodka and leaned against his desk, eyes boring into her.

"What do you think you're going to accomplish?" Nina said. "You're already compromised. You really think Beck is here alone?"

"Oh, Beck is it? On such personal terms." Leksik smiled.

"You might not think of people as human beings, Leksik, but I do."

"Most people are disposable, Nina. You will learn that in time."

"How did your wife die?"

Leksik stopped mid-drink and glared at her. "None of your business."

"Murdered? Is that what broke you? Losing the woman you loved?"

"You're such a romantic. You would love to think that, wouldn't you? Would it make my origin story tragically beautiful?"

"So you were born a broken thing?"

"Kindly shut your mouth or else I'll staple it."

Leksik slammed his drink. He wiped a dribble of vodka from his lip then picked up his phone and sent a message.

He said nothing for the next few minutes, just sat at his desk and stared out the window. Every moment stretched an eternity as Nina pictured Beck in that room with Yegor.

Finally, a knock broke the silence.

Leksik stood, cracked his neck and silently went to open the door.

Nina had to blink to take in what she saw.

"You wanted me?" Agent Shay O'Malley said.

"Kindly watch her. I have something to take care of."

O'Malley's eyes trailed the room and landed on Nina. For a moment, he deadpanned.

"Yeah, sure thing."

"I should be back in twenty minutes. Don't let her talk you into anything stupid," Leksik shot Nina a death glare before leaving the suite.

Nina exhaled with relief to see O'Malley's smug face.

"Holy shit, you have no idea how happy I am to see you," Nina said.

O'Malley rubbed his forehead. He didn't say anything and paced in a small circle.

"Shay, you all right? Undo this. Let's get the hell out of here. They have Beck."

"Yeah, I know."

Nina studied O'Malley. "You know? What the hell is going on? And wait, why did Leksik call you in here? How did...what's going on?"

O'Malley held up his hand. "Just stay calm, okay? Just give Leksik the information he wants, and he'll probably let you live."

Her jaw fell slack as she processed. "Sorry? Are you drunk or something?" Then the truth slapped her across the face. "Bastard."

He met her eyes. They were almost apologetic. But not almost enough.

"What did he offer you?" Nina said.

"Enough."

"What's a soul go for these days?"

"Don't know. What'd you sell yours for? Accounting for inflation, I think I got a fair market price."

Nina laughed. "Maybe Leksik, Katja, Luther were all right. People can't be trusted. Has it been from the very beginning?"

O'Malley said nothing.

"At least have the decency to be honest," Nina said.

"Yes. From the beginning. The sting was my idea. Leksik knew."

"And you let me walk my heels right into the viper pit."

"I knew you'd survive. Somehow, you always do."

"And Beck?"

"He was never supposed to be here. Fucker went off the rails. Thanks for that, by the way. Could have cost a good man his life."

"You sold us out to Leksik. You told him he was here and that I went to him."

"You should've been more careful. What were you thinking anyway? What was *he* thinking?"

"He trusted you. We both did."

"In my experience, trust is an overrated past time."

"What was your end game here, O'Malley? What were you trying to accomplish?"

O'Malley sighed and helped himself to Leksik's vodka. "Vahtra and Feinstein knew the DEA was getting closer. They reached out to me and suggested I run interference until they could get things cleaned up. No one was supposed to get hurt. You know as well as I do, Vahtra likes to keep a low profile."

"Until he starts removing appendages. How did they even know you?"

O'Malley slammed down the drink and poured another. "Old contact in LA."

Nina laughed. "You're dirty. Always have been. I should have known. There was always something off about you. And here I thought it was just blind arrogance."

"All part of the act." he smiled thinly.

"And Beck never knew you were dirty?" Nina said.

A glint of guilt flashed in O'Malley's eyes. "He didn't know."

"You can still fix this, Shay. Get me out of here. Let's go get Beck and get to safety. Then we can send the goddamn cavalry in."

O'Malley massaged his temples. His eyes looked weary, bloodshot. Was the weight of his betrayal breaking him down?

"No. I'm sorry but I can't. I don't want you dead, but my life and future mean more to me than yours. So if Leksik wants to kill you, I'm not going to stand in his way. You knew the risks."

"And Beck? You'll kill one of your own?"

"They won't kill him."

"Like hell they won't. And they'll kill you, too. You're

never getting out of this. None of us are. There are too many loose ends now. Leksik won't spare any of us."

"He and I have a deal."

"So you think he's going to let you witness the murder of a federal agent and just walk away?"

O'Malley hesitated.

"You're giving me a headache. Just be quiet." O'Malley paced. His body twitched, and he wrung his hands mindlessly.

Nina was wearing him down. "C'mon, Shay. You're not like them. This is too high a price to pay. I get dirty money. You put yourself on the line every day for shit pay. It's hard to resist. But innocent lives? Are you really willing to—"

"Jesus fuck, if I untie you will you shut up?"

Nina smiled. "Not a word."

He groaned. "What is it you think you're going to do?"

"Untie me. Give me your gun and we'll go get Beck."

O'Malley snorted a laugh. "Give you my gun? Cute."

"That way, if we're caught, you can play hostage."

"They're going to believe you overpowered me and took my gun?"

"Yes. Having met both of us, it's a reasonable conclusion."

O'Malley glared, but his hands went to the zip ties around her wrists. "You're insane, you know that?"

"Put it in your report."

He pulled out a pocket knife and slipped it through the plastic ties. They broke free and Nina whipped up her hands. O'Malley jumped back. "Settle down. We do this slowly. Don't lose your shit just yet, kitty cat."

They gingerly left the hotel suite and crept down the ornate corridors, trying to stay discreet. She had her arm around O'Malley lovingly, but the gun shoved right into his kidney.

"We're never getting into that room," O'Malley said.

"I'm willing to try."

"He likely has cameras all over these halls. He's already going to know you're gone."

She shoved the gun into him harder. "Then walk faster."

They picked up the pace as they moved down the hallway and into the maintenance room. They rushed into the elevator.

"Which floor was it?" Nina said.

O'Malley swallowed audibly. "All the way down."

Nina closed her eyes as she pressed the button.

Nothing had ever been so slow in its descent.

The elevator pinged like a gong signaling the start of a battle. The doors opened.

They were met by an unknown man in a suit. In a flash second, O'Malley manifested a gun and fired a silent shot into the man's forehead. The body thumped to the ground.

Nina blinked in horror. Then she looked to O'Malley. "You had two guns?"

"Don't be such an amateur, Nina. C'mon."

They hopped over the fallen soldier and ran down the corridor.

They drew near the room. Nina recognized the smell of bleach, the hum of a hotel backstage.

"He's in through that door," O'Malley said.

"Well c'mon then."

"He might not be alone."

"All the more reason to get there now."

Nina didn't wait for O'Malley and ran ahead.

She paused for a split second before clutching the door handle and pulling.

## 33

B eck's head hung limp, his shirt ripped open. Blood was caked around his mouth and down his firm torso. He was unconscious.

But he was alone.

Nina ran to him and frantically worked to undo the ties holding his hands behind his back. Her fingers shook as they tried to rip off the ties. O'Malley slipped in beside her and used his pocket knife to break Beck free. His arms fell to the side, and his body slumped. Nina caught him.

"Beck! Beck, wake up. We've got to go. Oh my God, please wake up."

Her body trembled as panic snaked up her spine. Her palms dripped. She looked around the room frantically. Then spotted something.

"Hold him up." She secured him in O'Malley's grasp then grabbed Yegor's bag of tools. She pulled out a vial of smelling salts.

She inhaled, then ran the compound under Beck's nose. He choked and snapped awake.

His body convulsed in shock, and his eyes went wild, their blue now a dark gray tempest.

Nina grabbed his face. "Beck, baby. It's me. It's okay. Can you stand?"

He blinked a few times, struggling for breath. Then he threw his lips against hers.

Nina fought down the overwhelming desire to cry and pulled him up.

"C'mon. O'Malley, help me."

"I'm fine," Beck said. "I can walk."

"Go out and turn right. There's another service elevator that will take you to the lobby," O'Malley said.

"Not coming?" Nina said.

"No. I'll take my chances here. Go. Get the hell out."

A question formed on Beck's face, but Nina put a finger to his lips. "I'll explain later." She turned to O'Malley. "Thanks for doing the right thing. I hope they don't kill you."

He smiled. "May we all live to die another day."

THEY SNUCK OUT OF THE INTERROGATION ROOM AND followed O'Malley's instructions. Nina's heart pounded so loudly she could hardly hear her own thoughts. Beck's arms were around her, holding her like it was the last time they'd ever touch. It almost had been.

The service elevator opened to the Casino lobby. The blips and dings of slot games and the laughter of drunks assaulted them. Sinatra crooned overhead.

Nina stood straight and took one careful step, then another. They were both a battered mess, but with any luck, people would assume they were just drunks who'd taken a spill.

Beck was struggling to stay upright as his adrenaline crashed, but Nina kept her arm around him, using every ounce of strength to steady him.

"Ma'am, do you need help?" A salt and pepper pit attendant stepped in front of them.

*Shit shit shit.*

"Um, no, we're fine, thanks," Nina said.

The pit attendant eyed her warily. "Your friend doesn't look fine."

"He um, he was in a fist fight down at the sport book. A few too many all around. Opposing teams. You know?" I just want to get him home."

The pit attendant studied them both for a moment, then smiled sympathetically. "The young guys let it all go right to their heads. Be safe. Have a good night and hope to see you again soon. Thanks for visiting The Royale Luxury Casino and Resort."

Nina smiled as best she could and moved toward the gilded entry doors, which seemed to shrink away with every step.

Finally, she felt the cold air slap her in the face.

Freedom. But not for long if they didn't run.

"Can't imagine you have a phone?" Beck said as they darted through the parking lot of the casino.

"No. I didn't have it on me when this all started. It's okay. There's a gas station on the corner of the main road. We can call Martinez from there."

They ran from the casino into the night. They would be chased momentarily she knew that. They had very little time to get to safety.

Beck was hanging in there, but he was going to need

medical care. He was fading fast, his broken body and mind fighting for survival.

They reached the road, but Beck stumbled. He toppled down, taking Nina with him.

"Fuck," he muttered.

"C'mon. Get up or we're dead."

"At least we'll die together. How poetic. Very romantic, you know."

"Shut your face, you idiot. The gas station is just another quarter mile or so."

"Probably owned by Leksik," Beck said as he pulled himself up.

"Probably, but they don't know who we are. Do you still have your badge?"

"Fresh out."

"Damn."

"Yep."

"It'll be fine. Just stay with me, Beck."

"Nina?"

"Hmm."

"I love you."

"Not the time, Graham. Not the time."

HALF WAY DOWN THE ROAD, NINA KICKED OFF HER HEELS AND opted to run barefoot. They reached the gas station on the corner and ran in and asked to use the phone. Taking in their battered appearance and her bare feet, the pimply teen boy behind the counter didn't offer any protest.

"What's Martinez's number?" Nina said.

Beck stared at her blankly. "I have no idea."

She relaxed the phone receiver and glared at him annoyed. "How do you not know that?"

"Because my body is going into fucking shock and I'm not sure I even know your name."

She groaned. "Fine, I'll just call 9-1-1."

Beck's hand snapped out and grabbed the receiver. "No, you can't."

"Beck, you need medical help now."

"Can't be an official record of any of this."

The counter clerk eyed them warily.

Beck sighed. "I know the station number. Hopefully Martinez is there. If not, whoever is on duty can get us through."

"Fine." Nina turned to the station clerk. "Have pain meds in here?"

Without a word, the teen pointed to an aisle of goods.

She ran and retrieved a pack of Advil while Beck took the phone and dialed.

"Shelley, hey, it's Beck. Yeah...I'm fine. No, I...hey, just listen for a sec, okay? Is Martinez at the station? Oh, thank God for workaholics. Put him on. Please. Yes, now. NOW."

IT SEEMED AN ETERNITY BEFORE THEY FINALLY SAW LIGHTS breaking through the darkness of the rural state line road. Finally, a black SUV pulled up and momentarily, they were headed toward safety.

Once the doors were locked, Beck's head hit the seat, and he passed out.

## 34

Nina sat beside Beck's hospital bed. He'd been sleeping for hours now, his body finally releasing its adrenaline and giving into fatigue. They'd done an examination on her as well and concluded she was beaten, but not broken. She should ice her shoulder and cheek and should stay overnight in the hospital for monitoring just in case. But she would likely be just fine.

An assisting officer had been kind enough to go by her house and bring her a change of clothes and her cell phone —her real one, not the one she'd allowed Yegor to confiscate. With her face washed and her own clothes— the stench of the casino scrubbed away—she was starting to feel like herself again.

It would take time, but they would recover from this. They would both have scars, but at least they were shared scars. Memories of suffering together. At least, she hoped that would be the case.

She stroked Beck's bicep, reveling in its grandeur. He was a specimen of a man. And they had tried to break him. They had tried to destroy something beautiful. For that, she wanted to make them pay. But there was nothing she could do now. She had tried, and she had failed miserably.

Now there was a bounty on their heads. If Leksik were insane enough to have Beck tortured, he wouldn't think twice about killing him. He no longer feared the American government.

Beck stirred. His eyes fluttered open.

"Hey there," Nina said.

"Hey. That's a sight I don't mind waking up to," Beck said, his voice croaking. She picked up the cup of water by the bed and tipped it into his mouth.

"How are you feeling?" Nina said.

Back smiled thinly. "Like I was tortured and run over by a truck. So, slightly better than I look. Sorry, Nina, but I think your friends are a little rough for me."

Nina tried to smile, but it hurt.

"It's weird how adrenaline can get you through so much and then the moment you're safe, the body just collapses," Beck said.

"The body is an incredible machine. But you're going to be fine. They didn't break anything that can't be fixed." She stroked his sweaty forehead.

He took her hand. His eyes ran over her, taking in her arm in a sling. "How are you?"

She shrugged. "As well as can be expected, I guess. I'm a little beat up. It's not broken, just pulled badly. God, Beck, I'm just so, so sorry. For everything."

"None of this was your fault."

"I should have known better than to think I could go in there and outsmart Leksik or any of them."

Beck stroked her hand. "It was O'Malley who fucked us, Nina. Not you. If anyone is to blame, it should be me. I'm the one who should have seen him for what he was."

"What the hell were you thinking, Beck, going in there alone?"

"I thought something needed to be done. I knew something was off."

She resisted the urge to slap him. "You didn't even tell Martinez. You went in there totally rogue. You know how dangerous that is?"

"Yes, I know. Maybe not my best decision. But at the time I thought O'Malley would have my back."

"You could have died." Nina felt her voice choking as a sob threatened to erupt.

Beck took her hand. "You think I'm so weak? I had days left in me."

Nina laughed through her tears. "Always playing the tough guy. God, I don't know what I would have done if I hadn't gotten there in time."

"Stop, Nina. Don't think like that. You did get there in time and you saved my life, woman. Come here." Beck pulled her close, and for a moment she let herself relax into his warm embrace.

"So now what?" Nina said, pulling away. "They're going to come after us."

"Yes, I imagine they will. We can have witness protection here within moments. We're going to be okay. We'll be safe."

Nina tossed her hair. "Beck, let's not fool ourselves. We've crossed the point of no return. There's no way we're ever going to be safe again."

"What do you suggest then?"

Nina bit her lip and contemplated all the options. "I don't know. I feel so helpless."

"Witness protection has kept some people alive for twenty years. It's an option."

"I can't imagine living like that. But I guess there isn't an alternative, is there?"

"Well, you could always do what you always threaten to do. Run off to Thailand. Marry a millionaire and live on a yacht." Beck smiled.

Nina laughed. "Yeah, well, you had to go and complicate that, didn't you? Would you go with me if I did? Just hypothetically speaking."

"Run off to Thailand and marry a millionaire? I'm not sure there's much of a market for a man like me. But maybe we can find a millionaire with an open mind," Beck said, grinning.

"I'm being serious, Beck. Millionaires aside, would you leave with me? Travel the world, hide in plain sight?"

Beck's grin faded. "Nina, I don't know. I can't think about this right now. This thing isn't over yet."

"You're right, I'm sorry. You need rest. I just feel like we don't have a lot of time."

He squeezed her hand. "We have more time than you think. Take a moment to breathe. When was the last time you slept?"

"I guess I'm overdue. We both are. I'm going to go get something to eat. Can I bring you anything?"

Beck shook his head. "No. I think I just need to sleep a little bit. The meds are something fierce."

Nina stood. "I'll make sure they keep you well guarded." She leaned in and kissed his lips gently, lingering for a moment.

She turned back and fixed his image to her memory before leaving the hospital room.

SHE WAS WALKING DOWN THE CORRIDOR, RUNNING THROUGH

scenarios in her head about the best next steps when her phone buzzed.

She jumped.

She almost didn't want to look. Slowly, she pulled it from her pocket. A text banner splayed across her screen. She unlocked the phone and breathed.

*Did you think we would let it pass? Call this number. Now.*

She traced the numbers with her thumb, not knowing what to do. She should just ignore it. Whoever it was, was just trying to scare her. They couldn't hurt her now.

But before she could make any decisions, it buzzed again.

*If you ever want to see Abby again, you'll call us.*

She sucked in a breath. Her vision blurred. Abby. Her niece. Just a baby. What had they done to Abby?

And as though she summoned it, her phone rang. She nearly dropped it. Cammy's number lit up the screen.

Nina's heart sank. She quickly swiped her phone and answered.

"Nina! Nina, they have her!" Cammy's voice spilled out, her terror traversing the distance.

"Cammy, slow down. What's going on?"

"They took her. My daughter. My two-year-old angel."

She didn't need to ask, but she did anyway. "Who, Cammy? Who took her?"

"You know damn well who did."

"When?"

"Moments ago."

Abby, sweet little angel-faced Abby with her chubby belly and wispy blonde hair. Her sweet giggles. Why? Why would they take her? But she knew.

Nina pressed her eyes closed, the world spinning.

"How?" Nina managed to say.

She felt Cammy's anger radiating.

"They broke in and took her. Men in masks. Just snatched her right up."

"Did they make demands, a ransom?" Nina asked.

"No, nothing. They just said we had you to thank."

Nina's heart contracted. This wasn't a ransom. This was retaliation. They had no intention of giving her back. This was a punishment to hurt her where it hurt most.

"Cammy, I—"

"Don't," Cammy broke in. "I don't want to hear it. But you will bring her back to me. Or so help me God, I will murder you myself."

"Cammy, call the police immediately."

"From what I understand, the police aren't going to do diddly."

"Just do it anyway okay? At least then you'll have protection."

"What happened Nina? Why would they take my baby? What did you *do* to them this time?"

Nina breathed in and out three times. "I don't have time to explain. But I will get her back, Cammy. I promise. I've got to go."

Before Cammy could say anything else, Nina hung up the phone.

There were certain wrongs Nina could abide in life. Certain people, she could stand getting hurt. She could suffer her own pain and loss. But she could not bear her family suffering for her mistakes. And especially not a child.

She thought of Abby and Jacob, those sweet little angels. They had birthday parties to host and trips to Disneyland, and summer vacations in Hawaii. They had stupid Christmas cards to make, and Little League games during which Cammy would sit in the stands and cheer them on with a cup of top-shelf vodka-spiked lemonade next to the other PTA moms. And they would all brag about their darling, perfect angels, and how they're so, so smart and really going places.

She thought of the stark dystopian tangent of another life. A family ripped apart by a cruel and vicious sadist who was only doing this out of spiteful revenge.

At that moment, Nina felt her entire world spin on its axis. She felt her body collapsing in on itself, her lungs struggling to inflate, her blood desperately trying to flow. Her bones felt like Jell-O.

She had minutes, possibly hours if they were lucky, before that child was on a plane headed to God knows where.

She stared at her phone, then dialed the number.

"I was wondering how long it would take you." The sharp female voice said on the other end.

"You bitch. Where is she, Katja?"

"She is fine. So sweet. She is here on my lap now. I've never liked children, but this one is quite lovely. She's just a baby, but there is always a market for little blonde babies. Especially American ones."

Nina pressed her eyes closed and breathed. No. There was no way that her innocent niece was being sold into slavery or to some family across the world.

"What do you want, Katja? Just tell me what you want in exchange. My life? You want me dead? Fine."

Katja laughed. "So noble all the time. I want nothing from you other than to watch you suffer. I think that is sweeter than your life."

"I will find you."

Katja laughed again, an eerie haunting melody. "We will see. Goodbye, Nina. I think I've had it with this country."

The phone went dead.

Nina's entire body throbbed as the rage bubbled up. She glanced to Beck's room. Did she tell him? No. Even if he wanted to help, there was nothing he could do. He was confined to a hospital bed.

Nina opened her phone and sent a text to one person she knew could help her.

*I'm going to need that passport.*

## The End of Book 2

Thank you for reading *All That Glitters*. If you enjoyed it, it would mean the world to me if you would please leave a review!

Don't miss *The Cat's Reprisal*, The Redemption Series Book 3.

# ACKNOWLEDGMENTS

*To Thomas, for helping me through this project from inception to finish.*
*I couldn't do it without you.*

A big thank you to my fabulous team! My editors Teresa Kennedy of Village Green Press and Hopey Gardner; my cover designers Peter and Caroline O'Connor; my fabulous beta reader, Emily; and the entire team at Florence & Reynolds

# ABOUT THE AUTHOR

Amanda J. Clay is a California native, currently residing in Denver, CO. When she's not creating fiction, she spends her free time plotting world adventures.

Do you have thoughts or questions about *The Redemption Lie?* I'd LOVE to hear from you! amandajclaybooks@gmail.com.

Connect with me below or visit me at amandajclay.com.

# ALSO BY AMANDA J. CLAY

**The Redemption Series**
The Redemption Lie
All That Glitters
The Cat's Reprisal

**Rebel Song Series**
Rebel Song
Rebel Rising
Rebel Fire

**Standalone**
Hollowbrook Haunting: A Paranormal Gothic Romance
Lies in the Darkness

41916941R00161

Made in the USA
San Bernardino, CA
06 July 2019